He was beautiful, Bethany realized. He was everything she'd ever wanted—inside and out.

"Why are you crying?"

"I don't know," she replied. "Just happy to be alive, I guess."

"You cheated death. Tears are not an uncommon reaction." Xavier captured her hand and kissed her knuckles. "Rest. I'll make camp."

He wanted to treat her like a girl? This time, she wasn't going to object. "Thanks."

Letting the breeze that rose from the gorge cool her, Bethany closed her eyes and listened as he pitched the tent and unpacked the minimum amount of gear needed for the night.

She knew the reason for her tears. It had nothing to do with cheating death and everything to do with Xavier. She had to tell him what she'd done. The lies. The money. *Everything.*

He wouldn't abandon her. He wasn't that kind of man.

Dear Reader,

One of the themes that runs through most of my books has to do with sisters or women who are as close as sisters. When one discovers that I have two of them, it's not a shocker. Though we live far apart, we get together whenever we can and call every week. I would do anything for them!

So when it came time to write the next Mercenary book, it wasn't a stretch for me to consider a "sister" issue. Of course, in this case, it's a tad different, especially when one adds FARC, aka *Fuerzas Armadas Revolucionarias de Colombia–Ejército del Pueblo* into the mix. An actual Colombian group, they kidnap hundreds of people every year. And I wondered what I'd do if they took one of my sisters....

Thus Bethany was born. A woman who will do what it takes to rescue her sister, Samantha, from FARC—including hiring Xavier Moreno. A mercenary who isn't just about the money, Xavier wants to save his country and his people from thugs like FARC. But is he strong enough to resist the pull of his own heart? You'll have to read the book to find out.

Sharron

SHARRON McCLELLAN
Mercenary's Promise

Romantic
SUSPENSE

 SILHOUETTE BOOKS

Recycling programs for this product may not exist in your area.

ISBN-13: 978-0-373-27647-9

MERCENARY'S PROMISE

Books by Sharron McClellan

Silhouette Romantic Suspense
Mercenary's Honor #1530
Mercenary's Promise #1577

Silhouette Bombshell
The Midas Trap #29
Hidden Sanctuary #114

SHARRON McCLELLAN

began writing short stories in high school but became
sidetracked from her calling when she moved to Alaska
to study archaeology. For years, she traveled across the
United States as a field archaeologist specializing in burials
and human physiology. Between archaeological contracts,
she decided to take up the pen again. She completed her
first manuscript two years later, and it was, she says, "A
disaster. I knew as much about the craft of writing as Indiana
Jones would know about applying makeup." It was then
that she discovered Romance Writers of America and began
serious study of her trade. Three years later, in 2002, she
sold her first novel, a fantasy romance. Sharron now blends
her archaeological experience with her love of fiction as
a writer for Silhouette Books. To learn more, visit her at
www.sharronmcclellan.com. She loves to hear from her
readers.

To Glennis and Heather.

I'd always come after you.

Chapter 1

"What do you mean the negotiations are finished?" Bethany Darrow leaned across Stephen Grimes's desk, her hand tipping a stack of papers, scattering them to the floor.

The lawyer for Tri-Continent Engineering looked at the mess, then at her. She didn't bother to apologize. "You are *not* finished. My sister is out in the jungle somewhere. Who knows what kind of hell FARC is putting her through? You can't just leave her there. You owe her."

Two years ago, a rebel group kidnapped Samantha. Her younger sister had been surveying a stretch of land for a pipeline for TCE, and then one day, she was gone. Taken by *Fuerzas Armadas Revolucionaria de Colombia—Ejército del Pueblo,* better known as FARC. And while they seized hundreds of people each year, making millions to support their radical militant army and increase their hold into the drug trade, this was *her* baby sister.

His expression placid, Grimes ran a hand over his thinning

gray hair, adjusted his tie and straightened his shoulders. "TCE doesn't owe Samantha anything. She's a contractor who knew the risks. Now calm down."

Tossing her dark brown ponytail over her shoulder to fall down her back, Bethany dropped into the expensive leather office chair and reined in her anger. Years of experience as a wilderness guide in southern Utah had taught her that an emotional overreaction in the face of a bad situation led to mistakes.

Grimes's office wasn't the Utah wilderness, but the principle applied. "You have to understand, you're our last hope." She pulled a picture from her wallet and flipped it toward Grimes. It was the last one sent by the kidnappers—via a released hostage—to show that her sister still lived. "We have proof of life. Recent proof. We're close to getting her back this time."

He didn't bother to look at the picture but pushed it toward her with the tip of his index finger. "I know this is frustrating. But legally, this is what's best."

"For whom?" Bethany snapped.

"For everyone," he replied.

God, what a lie.

He continued, "I didn't want this. I want Samantha to come home just as much as you do."

"As much as me? Not even close," Bethany countered, trying to wrap her brain around TCE's pullout from negotiations for her sister's release. "Why are you abandoning her after two years? To screw with us?"

Grimes glared at her. Despite his age, his eyes were clear and hard as lapis. "Of course not."

"Then why?" Bethany pressed.

He rubbed the back of his neck. "The agreements with Express Engineers broke down. Samantha might be *our* contractor, but she is *their* employee. If they were willing to pay part of the ransom and sign a statement admitting full responsibility, TCE might be willing to pay the rest as a goodwill gesture, but without that, my hands are tied."

Express Engineers—the company that sent Samantha to TCE. They were worse than TCE in that they claimed sympathy, but when it came down to action, they backed away.

Bethany clenched her hands into fists, afraid that if she didn't do something with them she might slap the lawyer. "So no one wants to admit responsibility and my sister is left to die in a no-man's-land of legalese."

Grimes remained silent. It didn't surprise her. To say much more might admit culpability, and that was not in the best interest of TCE.

And Grimes always did what was best for TCE.

"So what happens now?" she asked.

"The Colombian kidnapping task force is still working the case."

"And they've been so successful," Bethany said, with a snort of disgust.

Grimes sighed. "This isn't easy for me, either."

She picked up the photo off the desktop. The woman in the picture bore little resemblance to the sister she remembered.

Holding a newspaper dated from last week, she was thinner. Her mahogany hair was chopped shoulder length and bleached pale by the Colombian sun, the image a far cry from the long-haired, coiffed woman she knew. They'd beaten her as well, and even though it was the hundredth time Bethany looked at the picture, it still made her want to cry.

Next to Samantha stood Cesar, her sister's jailer. With his shaved head and clean clothes, he grinned as if posing for a portrait. *Bastard.* The sight of him made Bethany want to shred the picture, to erase his mocking grin from the world, but reason ruled.

She turned her attention back to Samantha. It was her eyes that upset Bethany the most. They were the same bright green as hers, but an unfamiliar fear filled them along with a weariness and a resignation that Bethany wasn't ready to admit plagued her, as well. At least, not yet.

Not even when Grimes and TCE decided to abandon her and her family.

Samantha needed her, she reminded herself. Her mother needed her. And she'd be damned if she was going to fail them. She'd rafted rivers that people claimed were death traps, and when she had reached the end, she'd screamed her success to the world.

TCE wasn't going to beat her. They were people. Politics. Nothing more.

Bethany kissed the photo before she slid it in the back pocket of her jeans. Hold on, Samantha. I'll get you out of there.

Standing, Bethany tugged at the edges of her pale green, well-worn T-shirt. "Don't worry about Samantha, Mr. Grimes. This situation isn't your problem anymore."

"I wish there was something I could do." Grimes stood and came around the desk. More than six feet tall, he towered over her with the top of her head reaching just below his shoulder. "What are you going to tell your mother?"

Bethany looked up at him. "My mother? I thought you knew."

They'd met with him at least once a month, if not more, since Samantha's abduction. He'd talked with them for hours on end, explaining the myriad issues surrounding an international kidnapping. Hell, he'd seen her cry. Grimes was an important and annoying part of their lives. It seemed odd that he'd missed something so monumental.

"Knew what?" he inquired.

"They operated last night and put her into a chemically induced coma to allow her brain to heal."

Grimes's cheeks turned red then paled as he realized the order of events. He clasped her shoulder with a wrinkled hand. "I am so sorry. You should have said something."

His hand still on her shoulder, Grimes led her to the door.

She shrugged him off. He voiced the right sentiments, but his actions spoke louder.

"What now?" he asked her.

It was a good question. On the upside, now that TCE had abandoned her, she couldn't hurt negotiations. Hell, there weren't any. There would be no more days spent by the phone waiting for a call. No one to give her false hope. No more sitting by her mother's bedside and lying to her—telling her that her youngest daughter would be coming home soon.

Bethany knew what she was going to do. She wouldn't listen to lawyers who told her to not interfere. She'd ignore the men and women paid to cover the company's ass. She'd do what she should have done the moment she found out that FARC took her sister—contact Angel and Fiona.

The ex-mercenary and his famous reporter wife had become good friends with her when she worked as a movie consultant on the same film as Angel. In a short time, she'd come to know and respect both for their tenacity and commitment to a variety of humanitarian causes. When the film had wrapped, the three parted as friends.

She didn't know how good of friends until Samantha was kidnapped—they were the first people who called her when it hit the news. They had a friend in Colombia, they told her. One who specialized in rescuing FARC kidnap victims.

But she'd let Grimes talk her out of hiring a mercenary. She'd believed the lawyer when he told her that negotiations were best. That if she were patient, her sister would be released.

Both she and Grimes had been fools.

No more waiting.

She might not have the seven hundred thousand dollars FARC wanted, but Angel and Fiona were on her side. Add a phone call and a plane ticket to Colombia and she'd get Samantha out. It was a crazy idea, but then so was the situation.

Besides, there wasn't another choice.

Bethany shrugged. "I'm not going to do anything. Talk to the embassy. Wait. Hope that the situation improves."

He looked down at her, suspicion in his eyes. "Nothing foolish though, right?"

Bethany looked up at him, not surprised at his perception. He knew her well enough to know who she was beneath the skin. "Of course not," she lied.

"Good. Don't." Still, he didn't seem convinced. "Let the Colombian government do their job."

Right. Like TCE did theirs? She wasn't putting her bruised faith in politics, corporations or foreign governments anymore. She'd put her faith in a specialist—someone who knew FARC and had beaten them before. Angel's friend.

Xavier Monero.

"Please, let him be the one I need," Bethany whispered.

As soon as she'd left Grimes's office, she'd gone home, gathered her files, her passport and called Angel to arrange a rendezvous between her and Xavier. He and Fiona had been happy to help though not pleased she was going to Colombia herself. Still, they had given her what she needed, and she'd booked the first flight to Buenaventura, a city on the coast of Colombia.

Twenty-four hours later she was jet-lagged and her jeans and white T-shirt smelled like old sweat, but she was at Rubies, Xavier's bar. It was a start.

Even though it was early in the day, music poured from a bar across the street, mixing with the chatter of the populace and the occasional shout of a street vendor. The sky was gray with signs of an impending storm, and the scent of the ocean mixed with exhaust from the cars.

Under other circumstances, she'd take the time to explore the tropical seaport. Learning to navigate new environments was both her job and her nature. But right now, there was business to attend to.

She slung her backpack over her shoulder, steeled herself and pushed open the door to the bar. The place was crowded with men dressed in blue and white sports jerseys. At the far end of the room was a wide-screen television showing a rugby game in progress. She pushed through the crowd toward the bar. The men didn't give her a second glance.

The bartender was young. Too young, she guessed, to be pouring alcohol, but then again, this was Colombia.

"*¿Hablas inglés?*" she asked, straining to be heard over the din as the men yelled at the television.

"A little." He smiled at her, the grin reaching all the way to his dark brown eyes.

"I am looking for Xavier Monero," she said. "Is he here?" She'd didn't bother to scan the crowd. Angel didn't have a picture of the mercenary, and Xavier wasn't to be found on the Internet.

The bartender gave her the once-over in reply.

Bethany fought the urge to roll her eyes, forced a smile to her lips and endured the ogling. "Well, is he here?" she echoed when his attention settled back on her face.

"He is in the back." The bartender pointed toward a door against the back wall and away from the television. "Getting more beer."

"*Gracias,*" she said and headed to the door. Someone on the television must have made a goal because the bar broke out in shouts and clapping. Hands over her ears, Bethany hurried into the back room without knocking and slammed the door behind her.

She leaned with her back against the door, and the first thing she noticed was the gun pointed at her forehead.

"*¿Quiénes son usted?*" the man holding the gun demanded.

Bethany froze, her eyes glued to the barrel of the weapon.

"*¿Quiénes son usted?*" he repeated, his tone insistent.

Bethany swallowed hard and reminded herself to breathe. *This is just like going up against a wild animal,* she told herself. *If you show fear, you're dead.* She forced her attention away from the weapon and met the man's gaze. His eyes were as black and hard as obsidian. His wavy, shoulder-length hair and strong jaw reminded her of Antonio Banderas from *Desperado.*

Handsome, she realized, if he didn't have a weapon aimed at her head. "I'm American," she responded, her voice quivering despite her intentions.

"That doesn't answer my question. Who are you?" he inquired in perfect, accented English.

"Bethany Darrow," she replied.

"What do you want, Miss Darrow?"

"Are you Xavier Monero?" Her attention slid back to the gun. She swallowed again. *No fear.* Despite the mantra, her knees began to shake.

"Why?"

Bethany met his eyes once again. She hoped he was Xavier. Even taller than Grimes, and with muscle upon corded muscle that loose jeans and a maroon work shirt did nothing to disguise, he looked like the kind of man capable of a rescue mission.

"I need your help." She took a deep breath. *Calm.* "If you don't mind, I'm getting a file. It will explain everything."

She let her backpack slip from her shoulder and down her arm. The metallic click of a gun being cocked froze her midaction.

"I mind. Dump the bag." He motioned with his gun.

She nodded and upended her worn pack without ceremony, scattering the spare clothes, toiletries and the files across the rough wood floor. Her spare panties ended up on top of the files. "I didn't check anything." She leaned down to retrieve her underwear and hide her heated face. "So I put in everything—"

"Keep your hands up," he interrupted.

"Of course." She straightened and put her hands back in the air, palm out but glared at him despite the gun. He didn't have to be a jerk about it.

He waved the gun at her. "Turn."

Bethany did a slow pirouette. "Happy?"

His attention still focused on her, a brief twinkle lit his black eyes. He brushed aside the pink bikini briefs and picked up the file folder, all business once again. "What's in here?"

"Everything I have on my sister's kidnapping," Bethany explained.

He didn't open it but scowled at her as if the information was the last thing he wanted to see.

Desperation washed over Bethany. Wasn't helping people his job? Shouldn't he show some interest? "Just read the file. Please. Angel said you would help. He said to tell you to call him if you didn't believe me."

"Angel sent you?" His scowl softened. "Why didn't you say that earlier?"

Once again, her attention slid up to the open end of the Xavier's weapon. "The gun pointed at my head distracted me."

He chuckled and lowered the weapon but did not put it away. "Have a seat." He nodded toward a small table at the back of the room. "Hands on top."

"Thank you," she said. The tension that twisted her gut eased, and she edged past him and sat down.

Taking the seat opposite her, Xavier left the gun on his end of the tabletop and within easy reach while he pulled out two years' worth of e-mails and articles. His attention split between her and the contents, she took a moment to examine the mercenary and his world.

The plain clothes were unexpected. Jeans? She had thought he'd wear black. Wasn't that what mercenaries wore?

Her gaze slid up his arms, past his shoulder and to the gap in the buttons that showed just a bit of his chest. No scars.

"Like what you see?" Xavier asked.

Her gaze snapped upward. He didn't look amused.

Nice going, Bethany. Once again, a heated blush colored Bethany's cheeks. "Sorry," she mumbled and adjusted her position to look around the room—better that than to be caught staring again.

Behind her, he rustled through the pages. His back room was smaller than she had expected but still large enough to have a six-burner stove and an automatic dishwasher against the longest wall. The other walls were dominated by cases of beer and various food items.

All as organized and clean as her kitchen at home.

It felt like a good sign.

"This is your sister?"

She turned around. Xavier held up the first proof of life picture FARC sent her over twenty-four months ago.

"Yes," she said, twisting to face him. "And I need you to help me get her back."

He nodded, sifted through photos and then stopped. Bethany swallowed hard again. It was a shot of herself and Samantha during their last Christmas together. The one where she'd taunted Samantha. She'd bragged about her cool movie consulting job then told her sister that engineers were boring. Dull.

Pushed and pushed until Samantha took the job in Colombia just to prove Bethany wrong. Now here she was. Working with a mercenary to bring her baby sister home and trying to be the big sister she should have been all along.

"Family is important," Xavier said, his gaze still locked on the photo. He ran a thumb over the photo, taking the smiles as truth. "They're everything. The ones who will stand by you no matter what."

When he looked to her, there was more than his belief in his black eyes. There was a pain she recognized because she saw it whenever she looked in the mirror. "FARC took someone you love, didn't they?"

He nodded. "My sister."

"I'm so sorry," she offered. "When?"

He handed her the picture. Her fingertips brushed his, sending an unexpected tremble up her arm that left goose bumps in its wake.

"You were close to your sister?" he guessed, closing off the topic of his life.

Fighting the urge to rub her arms, Bethany traced Samantha's profile. There was no way she was going to tell Xavier the truth—that she and Samantha had barely spoken to each other before she'd been abducted—not with his feelings about family. She couldn't take the chance he'd turn her down. "She's my best friend."

Xavier took a closer look at Bethany. Was she a FARC spy? She'd be the kind of woman they'd send. The smattering of freckles across her nose alleged easygoing tomboy, but the red strands that lit her deep brown hair and the emerald eyes spoke of a fire in her blood.

The combination was heady, but neither quality had persuaded him that she was who she said. It was the desperation in her eyes and his gut instinct that convinced him she was legitimate. Plus, she knew Angel.

His friend didn't hand out his name like party favors.

But rescue another kidnap victim? *Not going to happen. Not anymore.* Not even when it was a beautiful, mahogany-haired woman asking.

Still, he found himself reluctant to tell her to fly home. She seemed lost, and the guilt that surrounded her was almost tangible. Survivor's guilt, they called it. He felt it himself when he lay alone at night, watching the minutes crawl by until the sun rose and it was time to go to work.

Habit and curiosity urged him to continue to sort through the file on the table. He found a familiar clipping—a magazine article about FARC and their campaign of fear. Nowhere did it mention him, but it talked about what he and others like him did to help bring the kidnap victims home. He put the article aside, kept reading the rest of the file, and then stopped when he reached the e-mails. The first one was dated just over two years ago. "Why are you coming to me now? Why wait so long?"

"TCE was in negotiations with FARC, but those are dead as of a few days ago. I have money, but not enough to pay them what they're asking for. So, I came to you."

"How much do they want?"

"Almost three-quarters of a million dollars." Her voice choked and he looked up. Her green eyes watered, and for a moment, he thought she might cry.

Inside, Xavier winced. He never knew what to do when a woman cried. Offer comfort? Get them a drink? Beat someone up? Usually, he opted for staring at his feet in uncomfortable silence until they stopped.

She sniffed, but there was no torrent of tears.

Xavier breathed a sigh of relief and went back to the file.

"Will you help me?" she asked. "My sister is out there. I *need* you."

Need was a powerful emotion. A powerful word. It had been months since a woman looked at him with Bethany's intensity and uttered the word *need*. The sudden, unexpected vision of Bethany pressed against him, offering him solace with her touch and accepting it with his, made his mouth dry.

He closed the file. "I can't help you."

Bethany's eyes widened. "What do you mean, you can't help?"

He shook his head, hating his selfishness, but there was no choice. Not now.

She flipped open the folder, grabbed a picture and held it

out, demanding he take it. "Look at her. Look at Samantha and tell her you can't help."

Xavier took the photo. The girl, Samantha, had lighter hair, but her green eyes were twins to Bethany's. She held the requisite newspaper in her hand to show the date. "I'm sorry."

"Then tell me why. Tell *us* why," Bethany shouted. Her mouth quivered and he thought she might lunge across the table and try to force him into agreeing.

Xavier templed his hands in front of his mouth. She deserved to know that much and as much as he hated to admit it, he needed to talk to someone who just might understand. "I told you they have Eva."

"Your sister."

He braced himself. "FARC took Eva to teach me a lesson. Her ransom is over two million dollars—the amount of money they lost when I freed the hostages. There is no negotiation. No lowering the fee. But I'm close to the amount."

He hesitated, debating if he should even offer her hope. The desperation in her eyes made the decision. "Once Eva is free, perhaps I can help you. Until then, I can't take the chance."

"Would they kill her?"

He didn't think so. She was worth more money to them alive and FARC was all about the money. "No, but they'd up the ransom by that three-quarter of a million they want for your sister."

Bethany didn't respond.

Xavier leaned back, exhausted, knowing there was nothing more to say. He'd spent months hiding the pain of losing Eva and choking down the guilt at her abduction. The unexpected confession wearied him. He hadn't said that much to anyone about his situation. *Ever.* But Bethany was different. She was just as anxious. Just as lost. A companion in the fight to do what was right. He admired her conviction.

Bethany's skin paled, but her hands still shook. "Save Samantha and I will give you the money."

Xavier sat up at the offer. "You have a half million dollars?"

"I have that much," Bethany confirmed. She took his hand, squeezing his fingers. "Save my sister and I will give it to you for Eva."

Salvation. It would be easy to accept, but the speed of her offer begged caution. He pulled his hand from hers. "Give me the money now," he counteroffered. "When Eva is free I will save your sister."

Bethany shook her head. "It has to be now. No waiting."

Damn, she was stubborn. "I can't put Eva at risk."

"And I can't wait." Bethany leaned her head in her palms. "My mother is in the hospital in a chemical coma. I have less than two weeks before she wakes up. The one thing that keeps her going is the idea that Samantha is coming home. If she wakes up, and Samantha isn't there, I'll lose her, as well. I know it. We go after Samantha now, or I find someone else."

He wished he could help her. God knew he wanted too. "Two weeks?" He handed the picture back to her, unable to look at it any longer. "Even I can't help you in two weeks."

Bethany looked up and surprised him with a tight smile. "You can if I know where they're holding Samantha."

The location? Hope flared in his gut. It was insane to consider her offer. He couldn't jeopardize Eva's freedom, but if Bethany knew where her sister was kept, it might be possible to end this nightmare. Still, caution made him question everything and everyone. "How would you know such a thing?"

Bethany hesitated. "There is an online support group for people who have family and friends taken by FARC."

"I know of them." They'd even approached him, but he'd declined to join. His pain was private and his circumstances quite different.

"I've been a member for two years, and in that time, I've been talking to members off-line, gathering data, locations, troop numbers and timing of hostage movement, everything."

She chuckled but there was no humor in the sound. "A man named Cesar is holding Samantha, running the show and he is nothing if not predictable."

Xavier shrugged, unimpressed. "Unless you have the place and date of your sister's last location, you won't know where she is or where she will go next, no matter how predictable Cesar is."

Bethany held up the picture again. "This was given to me by a woman who was in the same camp as my sister." Bethany leaned over the table, intent. "I know where my sister is. I know when she is being moved, and I know where she is going next."

The hope in Xavier's gut flamed hotter and higher. "Where is she?"

Bethany edged back into her chair. "Take me with you and you'll find out."

Shock at the suggestion washed through Xavier. "What?"

She tilted her chin up, defying him. "You heard me. I'm going with you. And even then, you'll only receive partial directions until I'm sure you can't send me back."

Anger replaced shock. "You selfish little—" He clamped his mouth shut before he finished the sentence and crossed his arms over his chest to keep himself from grabbing her shoulders and shaking her until she gave him what he wanted. "You would put your sister at risk, *Eva at risk,* all because you want to play the hero?"

"It's nothing like that." Bethany's jaw tightened.

"Then what is it?"

"My reasons are my own and none of your business," Bethany remarked.

"They are if it threatens the mission."

"It doesn't. I can promise you that."

He believed her, but still, he hated secrets.

"This is my sister. My family," she urged. "Just like Eva is yours."

Family. He understood that. But she was inexperienced. One more person to worry about. "You'll slow me down if you don't get us killed first. Is that what you want?"

She held out her hands. "Here. Feel my hands."

Uncrossing his arms, he took her hands in his. Her skin was warm and her hands strong. "So?"

"Feel the calluses. I'm not some spoiled child you'll need to babysit. I'm a wilderness guide in Utah. I can help."

He turned her hand over. Her palms were rough. Used. This was not a woman who spent her days in a salon. He respected that, but it didn't convince him. "So you take rich people out into the forest for weekend camping. That doesn't change my decision. This is the Colombian jungle. We'll be moving fast. It's best if you stay behind."

Her cheeks blushed bright pink, and she yanked her hands from his. "What I do is a helluva lot more complicated, but I assure you that you can set me in the middle of nowhere— jungle or desert—with nothing but a knife and the clothes on my back, I'll walk out of there alive."

Obviously, he'd hit a sore spot.

She continued, "I wouldn't care if it was the top of Everest. My sister needs me, and I am going to get her back. You do this and take me with you, or I walk away with my money. It's as simple as that."

Why was it never easy? Every ounce of experience in him said she was a liability. But if this worked, if he freed Samantha without getting caught, then Eva would come home within weeks instead of months or even years.

Besides, it wasn't as if he had any more money coming in, no matter what he had said. He'd already called in every favor, every debt and still came up short.

"I'm not saying it will be easy," Bethany pressed. "But we have the information we need. They won't expect this. In. Out. Easy."

Simple? Easy? The woman was insane. If it were anyone else but Eva, he'd let Bethany walk away, but the guide had him by the short hairs. "I want payment in full. Up front. And proof the money is real."

"Half now. Half when we return," Bethany argued.

"Even if she isn't there. If you're wrong," he replied.

Fear flickered over Bethany's features, but she gave a slow nod. "I'm right."

He held out his hand. "I hope so. Agreed?"

She took his hand. Her grip was firm. "Agreed."

Chapter 2

He'd bought the lie. The ease with which she claimed to have five hundred thousand dollars had surprised Bethany. It had been a spur of the moment fib born from desperation, but now that she'd made the claim, there was no turning back.

Half a million? She groaned at the thought. She had three hundred thousand and barely that.

After their handshake in the back room and once she'd called her bank to wire him the two hundred and fifty thousand, Xavier had offered her a place to sleep in his room above the bar. She'd accepted with a relief that only an overnight flight to Colombia could muster.

Sleep wasn't easy with a guilty conscience nagging her and the gun under the pillow digging into her head, but she'd managed a few hours.

She shifted to her side and Xavier's creaky, throwback-to-the-fifties couch groaned in protest. Pulling her knees to her chest, she wondered how she'd become such an accomplished liar.

Her mother would be horrified. A lie in the Darrow house-hold was met with lack of dinner, the loss of privileges and on occasion, a mouthful of soap.

She knew the answer. Necessity. But it was such a big lie. The kind that people didn't forgive since it involved more than just her. It involved Xavier's family. And she understood the enormity of that responsibility better than most.

Still, she couldn't let it stop her. She couldn't dwell. She needed to move forward and remember that she did this for Samantha.

And for Samantha, she'd keep the lie, play it and make sure Xavier believed it, though she didn't think that would be needed. He'd believed her. Money did that to people. Made them believe what they wanted to.

What they needed to.

And now that he was "in," his attention was on the mission.

Once Samantha was safe at home, she'd find the money for Eva. "I won't let you down, Xavier," she muttered. She'd do whatever it took.

Despite the bravado, and the promise, she wondered if Xavier would forgive her once he discovered her duplicity.

Did it matter? Did she need forgiveness from a mercenary?

She needed to uphold her end of the bargain and nothing more. Gathering his money might take longer than he wanted or she claimed, but it would happen. Once she paid him off, she'd be back in the karmic black.

The bitterness in her mouth said otherwise and made her question whom she was trying to convince.

A noise outside the door made her pulse jump. Bethany's gaze shot over to the entry. "Xavier?"

The brass knob turned in response. Or was it FARC? She swung her legs over the edge of the couch, grabbing the gun as she rose. She pointed it at the door, hands shaking. "Who's there?" she called out.

The door finished its journey. Xavier stood beneath the frame. "Who do you think?"

His exasperated look told her that he was more concerned that she'd shoot him by accident than on purpose. He strode across the room and twisted the gun from her grip. "Never point a weapon at me. Especially my own."

Bethany stared at her empty hand. "Sorry."

"Expecting someone else?" he asked, setting the gun on the arm of the couch. The apartment was one large room with not much more than the couch, a wooden table with four chairs, an overflowing bookcase and an assortment of rugs that clashed with each other.

"FARC?" he continued.

She shrugged, embarrassed.

He opened the miniature refrigerator that just fit beneath the table and pulled out two bottled waters. "If a known FARC member arrived here, you'd hear gunfire." Handing a bottle of water to Bethany, he gulped the other down.

"Did you get any sleep?" he inquired, tossing the empty container across the room and hitting the wastebasket dead-on. "I need you ready to go and frosty."

"Frosty?" She rolled the bottle between her palms.

"Coolheaded. Prepared."

"I slept some," she answered.

"Thinking about Samantha?" he asked, his voice dropped, softened.

She nodded. It felt good to tell the truth, even a little truth.

His hand moved toward her and, for a heartbeat, she thought he might twine his fingers through hers. Pull her close. Comfort the sad sister. It was what most men would do. Well, most men who wanted to get into her pants.

She suspected that Xavier wasn't like most men, which both scared the crap out of her and sent a current of excitement that started in her belly and spread outward.

But his hand stopped midway, angled sideways and the movement transformed into a disappointing muscle-stretch. "If the information is as good as you say, we'll get her back," he concluded.

"It's good," she assured him. "It took years to compile." Opening the water, she drank a mouthful, the chilled liquid waking her like coffee couldn't. "I'm surprised the government doesn't have it. All they have to do is talk to the support group."

"Taking FARC on has never been their priority. When they do and they get their asses handed back to them, that's bad for public perception. Makes them appear weak."

Xavier's mouth turned downward, and his hands clenched into fists at his side. "So they ignore them, instead."

Bethany shifted from one foot to another in the face of his anger. One day, soon, he'd look at her with that same mixture of disgust and resentment.

The thought made her ache.

And still, she couldn't let it stop her.

"So what's next?" she queried, setting the water on the floor next to the couch and changing the subject for both their sakes.

"I've been thinking about that," Xavier commented. He reached for her again, but this time his hand didn't stop. He took her hand in his. "Bethany." He said her name like a lover, his accent heavier than usual. His thumb stroked her palm and the warmth of his touch spread through her, making it hard to breathe. "I want to ask you again to stay behind. Let me do my job."

Bethany froze. "What?"

He leaned toward her. So close that his breath brushed her neck, stroked her like a lover's touch. "Give me the location. I'll get Samantha and I can have one of my men begin talks with FARC to return Eva. Within a week, we can both have what we want. Our sisters will be home. Safe. All you have to do is wait here and let me do my job."

Bethany leaned back, shocked. Did he think she was so

weak that a simple seduction could change her mind? She gave him a pointed look. "Oh, my God. You are good."

He raised a dark brow in question.

She scooted back on the couch, breaking his hold on her. "You are trying to play me."

"Play you? What does that mean?" Confusion darkened his eyes.

"Play me. Use your *charms* to get me to do what you want." She jumped to her feet and paced across the small room.

"I want you to do what is best for everyone involved," he insisted.

Bethany stopped at the far side of the room and pivoted to face Xavier, hands on her hips. "Then ask. Don't sit there and try to woo me, thinking that it'll make me more pliable. I'm not that shallow or stupid."

He glared at her, all charm gone. "You are inexperienced and yet want to take on FARC. Already, your intelligence is in question."

"Do you think insulting me will change my mind?" Bethany snapped.

His jaw clenched tight, the muscles in his neck visible beneath the skin as he worked to regain control. "I am asking now. No *woo,* as you requested. Stay here. Let me do my job."

Samantha was her responsibility and neither insults nor charm were going to deter her from finding her. Bethany shook her head. "You know the agreement. I go or the deal is off."

Xavier rose and crossed the room, stopping inches from her and invading her personal space. She didn't step back. If he wanted a battle of wills, he'd get one.

Toe-to-toe, his breath washed over her skin, but it was no longer a caress. Instead, the heat of his anger scorched her.

She met his hard gaze with her own.

"As you wish," he muttered. "How long will it take to reach Samantha? In and out?"

Bethany went over the map, noting the landmarks—crevases, waterfalls and rivers—and estimating how long it would take a skilled team to navigate them. Two days in. Two out. One extra in case it all went wrong. "Five."

Still gazing into her eyes, he pressed a piece of paper into her hand. "This is a hotel just outside the city. Make a reservation for an extra-long weekend."

"Will that be enough time?"

"Plenty. We just need to make FARC think I am there. That is all."

He was the expert. "Okay."

"Make the reservation for two. King-size bed. Jacuzzi tub. Don't forget the champagne."

"More *woo?*" She crammed the paper into her pocket.

"Woo?" His slow, seductive smile sent a wave of heat through her gut, scaring up unexpected butterflies.

Suddenly, the thought of woo and Xavier didn't seem as irritating as it did seconds ago. What was he like when he was with a woman? Tender? Fierce? Both? She swallowed back the desire to find out. "No woo. Please."

His smile died. "We need a cover story for a few days. FARC is everywhere, waiting for me to screw up. I can't give them the opportunity." His fingers slid up her arm. "Use a different name for yourself. I don't think they know who you are and we want to keep it that way."

His hand slowed at her shoulder. "They must believe we're lovers."

Bethany fought her urge to lean into his touch. "I can do that," she confirmed, her voice half an octave higher than normal.

"Can you?" His hand slid to the back of her neck and he pulled her closer until their lips were inches apart. "I know how the wooing makes you angry."

"It does," she whispered, captivated by his caress and

both wishing he would stop teasing her and wishing it would never stop.

He breathed her in, his lips a breadth from hers. Then he released her. Bethany stumbled forward, catching herself before she fell into him. His touch turned her into an idiot. How was she going to survive spending time with him in a hotel? Or even the jungle?

"We leave at sunset." He stopped, hand on the doorknob. "Keep your secret, but I need a starting point for the team."

She nodded, grateful to get back to business. "We'll meet three kilometers south of San Pedro on Highway 25. From there, we take dirt roads to here." She pointed to her first reference point on the map. "Then we hike."

"Be ready." He stepped into the hallway. The sounds of the bar filtered up the stairs then disappeared as he slammed the door shut.

Bethany stared at the closed door and touched the back of her neck where Xavier's hand had rested. Her skin was still hot. Tingly. *Woo.*

"Jerk."

Bethany sat in the open window, hating the downtime as she waited for Xavier to do whatever it was he did. It gave her mind too much time to think and worry. Was her mother doing well? She was still in the coma, to be sure, but there were so many potential complications that came with the risky procedure.

And how was Samantha? Was she outside? Was she chained inside a hut? What were they doing to her baby sister?

She missed them both, so much. Bethany wiped her tearing eyes. Damn, she didn't like to cry and she hated missing people. "I'm coming for you. I promise. Just hang in there. And we'll be together again. All of us."

"She'll be home soon," Xavier declared, his low voice just over her shoulder.

Startled, Bethany jerked and grabbed the window frame to keep from falling out. "I didn't hear you come in."

"I know." He held out a hand to help her down from the ledge. "Next time, you should keep your attention on the door."

"How long have you been there?" She wiped her eyes again. The only thing worse than crying was Xavier seeing her cry.

"Long enough," he observed, his hand still out.

She gazed at it not sure what it would signal if she accepted his offer of assistance, no matter how small. Would he see that was weakness? Or a sign they were a team?

She took it. His hand almost swallowed hers. His skin was rough but warm. She hopped down from the ledge. "I made the reservation. I got the honeymoon suite. My treat."

"Who's wooing who?" He chuckled. His hand tightened before he let her go.

Surprised, she smiled back. It was good to see he had a sense of humor or it would be a long trip into the jungle. She gave an exaggerated shake of her head. "I promise to not seduce you."

"That's disappointing," he murmured. Xavier's gaze dropped to her feet and then worked his way along her body, his unexpected appreciation as hot as his touch.

No squirming this time, Bethany steeled herself, chin up and back straight. No turning into a gibbering idiot. Let him look.

His eyes locked with hers. Glittering and dark, they offered a dare. To do what, she wasn't sure, but she knew a dare when one stared her in the eye.

And she knew desire. His eyes drank her in and offered her solace…if she dared accept.

She broke their gaze, took a step back and bumped into the windowsill. "We should leave."

"Agreed." A slow smile curved his mouth. There was no desire behind the smile now. There was something else. Something she recognized in herself. The "I win" grin.

Dammit. She'd underestimated him and his desire to succeed. She wouldn't make that mistake again. She wrapped her arms across her chest.

Xavier's grin widened. "You will be happy to know that I have already laid a foundation for our weekend." Leaving her at the window, he walked to his dresser, opened drawers and stuffed clothes into a small duffle.

"How so?" she asked, kicking herself for giving him the metaphorical upper hand.

"I bragged to the bar," he explained. "Told them all about you, my new lover, and how we were going to spend the weekend naked. And that it might involve food. Possibly props."

Bethany's eyes widened. "My cover is a slutty whore?"

"Isn't 'slutty whore' redundant?"

"Fine. Whore." She buried her face in her hands.

Xavier laughed. "Not a whore. Let's go with *easy*."

She peeked at him between her fingers, wishing she didn't need him.

"What did you expect?" he asked. "We needed a cover. This one works. No one will question us."

She dropped her hands. "I know, but I don't have to like it."

He cocked his head. "Seems like we both have to do things we don't like."

"Looks like," she replied.

Xavier held up a gun. "Do you prefer the .325 or the 9 millimeter?"

Bethany hesitated. It wasn't as if she'd never shot a gun. She'd even shot the occasional animal when necessity demanded it. This was different. This was to protect herself from the members of FARC.

Despite the fact they were the enemy, the thought of shooting a person was unsettling.

That didn't mean she wouldn't do it. "The nine," she

decided, forcing her voice to remain steady. She could shoot the larger caliber but her aim would suffer. Better to go with accuracy.

Xavier nodded, tossed two of each plus holsters into the duffle and tied it shut. *"Vamanos, mi amor,"* he announced, with overemphasis on the *amor.*

She didn't speak much Spanish. Most of what she knew she gleaned from Shakira or Ozomatli music, but knew it was time to leave and play the part of Xavier's lover. "Jackass," she muttered under her breath as she picked up her pack to follow.

Xavier opened the door for her, flashing his "I win" grin at her as she edged past him in the tight stairwell.

He thought he won? Let him think it. She'd pay him back, and when she did, he'd regret toying with her. She smiled back with as much sarcasm as she could convey and headed down the stairs.

Chattering, the clink of glasses and the blaring of a Spanish television show increased as she grew closer. But when she stepped into the room, it went silent with all eyes on her.

Behind her, Xavier made a comment in Spanish. For a moment, she thought the crowd of men might cheer.

Bethany raised her hand in a self-conscious wave and headed forward, wishing the normal conversation level would resume before she melted into the floor from embarrassment.

Instead, there were winks, nudges and blatant stares as the crowd parted like the Red Sea around her.

She'd have preferred cheering.

Tightening her grip on her pack, she reminded herself this was for Samantha and held her head high as she walked the gauntlet with Xavier behind her.

She passed a man dressed in a black and gold jersey and he whispered something in Spanish to the man next to him. Laughter followed. Whatever he said, it wasn't complimentary.

Xavier slapped her on the butt.

Bethany stopped in her tracks. There was providing cover and there was overkill. Smacking her butt fell into the latter. The crowd's laughter stopped as if cut off by a knife.

Slowly, she faced Xavier. His smirk went all the way to his eyes and fueled her growing anger.

He thought that he'd make her squirm? That he was going to beat her? She'd show him what a Darrow girl was made of. Her gaze locked with his, Bethany set her backpack at her feet.

Xavier's smirk shifted into unease and hesitation. He held his hands palms out to show he was teasing. *"Lo siento, mi amor. Lo siento."*

An apology? If so, it wasn't enough. Not by far. She stepped into his space. He didn't back away.

Good. She wanted this lesson to be up close and personal. Grabbing the front of his shirt, Bethany pulled herself upward until her mouth was level with his. "For the audience," she whispered as she pressed her lips against his.

Xavier stiffened and for a breath, Bethany thought she'd won. That he'd break the kiss. Then his hand snaked around her waist. He pulled her tightly against him, claiming victory. Or trying to.

Like hell. This was her game.

Around them, the crowd roared in approval, but the pounding in Bethany's ears overshadowed their laughter.

Bethany rose on her toes, wrapped her arms around Xavier's neck and traced his mouth with her tongue. He countered by nipping at her lower lip.

Warm heat flushed outward from her middle, making her breathe harder. *Bastard.* She increased the pressure of her kiss, pressing herself against him while she teased him. Tasted him.

He didn't relent but lifted her until her feet left the floor, and she dangled in his arms.

The heat between them cloaked her like a blanket, melting her, but she refused to relent. She wasn't going to lose. Not when she'd started this game.

If she didn't, she'd never live it down.

"Señorita!" Someone tugged at both her and Xavier. He lowered her to her feet and broke the kiss. Laughing, the bartender shook a set of car keys and said something that she couldn't understand.

She made a mental note to learn Spanish when she returned home.

Xavier snatched the keys. "Time to go," he said, his voice rough.

Agreed. Bethany fought the urge to fan her face and picked up her backpack instead. Around them the crowd continued to hoot and cheer, the cries following them out into the street.

The door swung shut behind her and Bethany took a deep breath, as the cooling night air washed over her. With Xavier in front of her leading the way, she traced her still tingling mouth with the tips of her fingers.

She wasn't going to do that again. While she didn't think Xavier won their little public power struggle, she wasn't sure she could lift her arms in triumph, either.

"Don't get any ideas," Bethany indicated as soon as the bellman left. "You're sleeping on the couch."

Xavier tossed his duffle and Bethany's backpack on a bed big enough for four. Bethany hadn't been kidding when she had said she'd booked them the honeymoon suite. The sitting area offered an overstuffed, deep blue couch, a fireplace and champagne in a bucket with crystal glasses waiting for them. "Ideas? I wouldn't dream of it," he lied, knowing he'd do just that.

Kissing the guide in the bar had been a cross between hand-to-hand combat and foreplay. A weird erotic mix that left him wanting more.

"You sure?" Bethany asked, taking a seat at the end of the bed. "You seemed more than enthusiastic earlier."

Little minx. She thought she was so clever. "Positive," he proclaimed, sitting next to her and falling onto his back. "Because we're not staying the night."

She twisted around, her brows arches. "What?"

"I told you this was cover, nothing more," he repeated. "There will be someone to take our place in an hour, and then we will leave through the back door."

"Oh." She didn't look convinced.

"As long as the night staff doesn't see them, it's fine." While not a perfect plan, it was simple, and it was the simple ones that garnered success.

Sitting up, Xavier dumped his duffle bag onto the bed. There wasn't much inside. Dark shirt, black military-issue pants and their guns. "I hope you brought more clothes than what you're wearing."

Her upper lip curled. "It's not my first rodeo."

Touchy. Touchy. Xavier ducked his head to hide his smile. "Good. Change now and remember that whatever you're wearing, you'll be in it for the next few days."

Xavier pulled his shirt over his head as she picked up her pack and went to the bathroom.

She kicked the door shut behind her, but not before he caught a glimpse of her pulling her own shirt off, giving him a view of her strong, but feminine, back.

He imagined what she looked like as she continued to undress…standing in nothing but bra and panties. Strong lean muscles stretching. Soft skin turned pale in the light. Her dark hair undone and reaching to the middle of her back, begging for his touch.

"*Dios mío,*" he muttered. Thinking of Bethany naked was not going to help in this mission. In fact, it would do quite the opposite.

Forcing himself to focus, he grabbed a black, long-sleeved shirt and slid it on. Over that, his shoulder holster. Then black fatigues.

When Bethany emerged from the bathroom a few minutes later, he was dressed and waiting for her.

She wore a long-sleeved, black T-shirt as well, paired with black cargo pants not unlike his. Low on her hips was the holster he'd given her, a weapon on the side of each firm thigh.

He'd seen women carry guns before, but he'd never considered them sexy. Seeing Bethany made him reassess the decision. "It seems we shop at the same places," she noted. "Nice shoes."

He glanced at her feet. She wore black Doc Marten boots that were twin to his.

"Looks like," he concurred.

Her mouth turned up in a broad smile. The first real one he'd seen, he realized, since she'd walked into his bar this morning. And it transformed her face into something akin to angelic.

"What now?" she prompted, walking past him and stuffing her other clothes into her pack. "We wait?

He noticed that she'd braided her hair down the back and tied it with a strip of leather. A kick-ass angel. "We give the staff something to remember." He patted the bed next to him. "We make love. Loud."

Bethany's smile fell, and she crossed her chest with her arms, transforming from angel to annoyed imp. "Excuse me?"

"We act. We sell the lie," he said with a chuckle. "What did you think I meant?"

Her shoulders relaxed and she let her arms drop. "It's hard to tell with you."

She made it so easy to tease her that it was almost impossible to resist, but he promised himself to try. He patted the bed again. "Let's do it."

"This," she corrected. "Let's do this. We are not doing *it*." She walked past him and sat on the bed, facing the headboard. "A little help?" she requested, glancing at him over her shoulder.

He gave a nod of acquiescence and knelt next to her. Hands pressed against the heavy wooden frame, they pushed it against the wall, making it thump. "Again." Xavier said.

They pushed it again. And again. "Make some noise," Xavier urged. "Are you always this quiet in bed?"

Bethany gave him an exasperated sigh. "Give it to me," she cried out. "Give it to me *hard*."

Xavier choked on a laugh and glanced at Bethany. A smile lit her face. The angel was back. And it was laughing. "Sorry," she said, her voice low. "You said you wanted noise."

"I did ask," Xavier replied, a little stunned at her choice of words. Damn, but she was a constant surprise. Of all places to find amusement, he didn't think it would be here. On a bed. Especially when the thought of anything physical with him seemed to make her angry.

She gave a loud realistic moan. "Oh, God, Xavier. Oh, God."

Too realistic. Once again, the thought of Bethany naked washed over him. Her soft skin caressing him. Her long hair tickling his chest as she worked her way down his body.

Dios mío indeed. Xavier gave the headboard an extra hard push.

"You might want to make some sound," Bethany said.

"Men don't make sounds," he replied. He was more of a whisper-in-the-ear kind of man.

"You're the one that said we needed to be noticed. Unless you're scared."

The taunt was obvious but struck hard. "You would call me a coward?"

"No," Bethany objected, smiling. "Just saying that I'll do whatever it takes and I'm not so sure about you."

Xavier narrowed his eyes. How could he have ever thought the woman next to him was an angel? "I'll do whatever it takes," he assured her. With one arm, he pulled her close. "Whatever it takes," he whispered into her ear.

Despite the sound of the headboard thumping against the wall, he heard her breath catch.

Someone knocked on their door.

Xavier released Bethany and drew a weapon with the other hand, ready for a fight.

Chapter 3

"Your contacts?" Bethany whispered, working to keep the tremble from her voice.

Xavier held a finger to his lips for silence and rose from the bed. Bethany drew both her weapons to cover him, her hands shaking at the thought of a gunfight.

"If so, they are early," Xavier replied, edging towards the door. "And one can never be too careful." He held a hand out, motioning her back. "Stay there."

"What are you doing?"

He took a position to one side of the entrance. *"¿Quién es?"* he called out.

"¿Quién usted piensa? Absolutamente siendo estúpido y abra la puerta."

Xavier glanced toward her again, the message in his eyes louder than words. *Be ready.* Still standing to the side, Xavier opened the door.

A man waited in the hallway. He wore jeans, a maroon button-down shirt and mirrored sunglasses despite the fact it was now night. His hair was trimmed an inch or two shorter than Xavier's. But they were close enough in appearance to pass as brothers as long as the lighting was dim and no one looked too close.

Behind him, his companion shifted into view. For a moment, Bethany forgot to breathe. With her deep brown hair, easy smile and green eyes, the woman could be Samantha.

Or herself.

The man stepped inside, glanced at the gun and smiled. "Xavier!"

Xavier holstered his weapon and Bethany holstered hers with a sigh of relief. "I take it these are our replacements?" she asked, walking forward.

"You take it right," Xavier replied. "Bethany, this is Joaquin and Daria. They're with RADEC."

Revolucionarias Armadas de Colombia. Fiona had told her about them. Dedicated to bringing freedom to Colombia, its members were once considered rebels, but now they worked with the government. Xavier had been one of their leaders but left to dedicate his time to recovering FARC hostages.

"You're early," Xavier pointed out, sweeping his hand to the couch. The couple sat down. "Do we have a problem?"

Joaquin held up his fingers a few inches apart. *"Un poco."*

"English, please," Xavier instructed as he paced across the room. "What is happening?"

"We have word that FARC is sending a spy to watch the hotel," Joaquin reported, his expression grim.

"How do you know they haven't already arrived?" Xavier asked.

"They didn't figure out which hotel until a while ago. But now that they know, they aren't wasting time."

Bethany went cold. She knew they'd be watching Xavier but

thought they'd get a little lead time. She supposed she should count them lucky that they got wind of there being a spy at all.

Joaquin continued, "You need to go before they arrive, or it will be impossible to get away without being spotted."

Xavier stopped pacing and went to the bedroom. When he came out moments later, he held Bethany's backpack in one hand and a jacket for himself in the other. He tossed her gear to Bethany.

She caught it midair and slung a strap over her shoulder, carrying the bag like an oversized purse. Untucking her shirt, she pulled it down to hide the weapons at her side.

Daria said something in Spanish and Joaquin replied. Bethany felt for the girl. She seemed to be in the same boat— albeit for English—when it came to the language barrier and Bethany sympathized with her frustration at not knowing what was going on.

The RADEC pair rose. This time, Daria addressed Xavier in Spanish too fast for Bethany to understand even a single word. She handed him another set of car keys.

"*Gracias.*" Xavier kissed the girl's cheeks then put his jacket on. "Joaquin, enjoy the room and try not to spend too much of Bethany's money."

"No promises," Joaquin teased with a slight smile.

"Let's do this," Xavier said. Opening the door, he glanced down the hallway. "Clear." He motioned for Bethany to follow. She hurried behind him.

"Good luck," Joaquin said.

Bethany paused before she shut the door. "Thanks."

The carpeted passage was empty with the occasional muffled conversation filtering through the walls. Once again, Xavier held a finger to his lips and pointed down the hall to the lit exit sign. Bethany nodded. Side by side, they moved with a pace that was closer to a power walk than a stroll.

Once there, Xavier didn't hesitate but pushed through the

exit, pulling one of his guns as soon as the door closed behind them. Bethany did the same. Treading through the dark, they made their way down the stairwell, the occasional shuffle of a footstep breaking the dim silence.

Bethany's skin prickled in anticipation. She wouldn't feel safe until they were away from the hotel and in the jungle. Panthers and bugs she could deal with, but FARC spies made her jumpier than she had ever imagined.

Two floors below them, a door squealed and a swatch of light illuminated the darkness of the stairwell. Xavier stopped at the third-floor landing, one hand on the door ready to exit.

Two male voices echoed in the stairwell. They spoke in Spanish, but after a few seconds, Bethany caught a word she understood, *Xavier.*

FARC. She needed to buy lottery tickets. Adrenaline surged through her. For a moment, she thought her pounding heart might beat out of her chest.

Xavier yanked open the door to the third floor, and it squealed on its hinges. Behind them, the footsteps in the stair-well sped up.

"Hurry," Xavier said, stopping to hit the elevator button as they sprinted past.

Bethany slowed, but the elevator doors remained closed. "We need an open room," she said, not knowing what she would do if discovered. "Bathroom. Another freaking stairwell. Something."

They ran down the hallway, and Xavier herded her towards a door with a picture of a woman on it. They hurried inside a small room filled with buckets and brooms. A maid's closet.

Xavier clicked the lock and they crouched down in the small room.

"Think they'll fall for it?" she whispered, trying not to sneeze as the smell of bleach and air freshener tickled her nose.

"As long as they don't find us, they'll assume it was a guest that went into a room. Why think otherwise?"

She hoped he was right. If not, they were screwed. Samantha was screwed. And so was Eva. Outside, the elevator dinged its arrival, and the squeal of the third-floor exit door told them their pursuers were close. Bethany strained to hear the FARC spies and caught a muffled shuffling coming toward them, then past their hiding place. She started to rise. "We should go."

"Not yet," Xavier murmured, his hand on her shoulder. "Give them a minute."

"What if they find us?" she asked.

"We do what we have to," he said, his voice flat.

He meant kill them. Her stomach tightened.

"I told you it might come to this," Xavier reminded her.

He had, and a part of her wished she'd taken him up on his offer of leaving her behind. To accept Xavier's offer to save Samantha. It was his job. What he did.

Let him kill the bad men.

But Samantha was her sister, her responsibility and she couldn't just sit back and wait. Not even when she wanted to. "I'm good," she replied, her voice almost inaudible.

"Can I count on you to pull the trigger if it comes to that?" he asked.

She'd already traveled to Colombia and hired a mercenary. What were a few bullets? But the thought did nothing to quell the butterflies. "I'll do whatever I have to in order to save my sister."

Taking her hand in his, he kissed the knuckles. "I believe you."

For a split second, warmth replaced the cold fear that covered her. A click sounded as someone on the other side of the door tested the lock. The cold returned.

Xavier dropped her hand, and the whisper of metal and plastic against leather as he pulled his gun made her heart beat even harder.

Whoever stood outside yanked with more force, but the door held.

Go away. Go away. She chanted the mantra in her head. There's nothing here. Just us mops.

More voices caught her attention. FARC reinforcements? At this rate, there would be an entire militia out there.

Whoever was yanking on the door ceased pulling and muffled voices became audible. A minute later, the voices faded.

"What happened?" she muttered. "What did they say?"

"Room service came by. They wanted to know what our friends wanted."

Bethany sighed in relief and smiled in the dark. The air shifted as Xavier stood, pulling her to her feet. "Let's move. They might return and we want to be long gone if they do."

It was almost midnight when Xavier drove Daria and Joaquin's car, a beat-up, cherry-red Mustang, off the side of the road and into a clearing. He cut the engine.

"This is it?" Bethany asked. They were perched on the edge of the jungle with not a city light or body in sight.

"It's where you pointed at on the map," Xavier clarified, getting out.

Bethany stepped into the night and breathed deep. The smell of earthy decay and night-blooming flowers had replaced the acrid scents of the city. She stretched, working the kinks out of her back from the long car ride and enjoyed the silence.

Jungle or desert, the great outdoors was where she belonged.

She wished she'd arrived under better circumstances. "How long before your men get here?" Bethany inquired, eager to get moving.

"Soon." Opening the trunk of the car, he set her backpack on the ground, pulled out a large piece of cloth and handed her a corner. "Help me with this."

It was camouflage netting she realized. Not cloth.

Together, they unfolded it, walking the net over the car.

Gathering branches, brush and leaves, they covered the vehicle until it looked like a pile of vegetation, as long as no one took the time to look too close.

"*Ese.* We wondered when you would arrive," an unknown voice said.

Bethany pulled her weapon, pointing it into the dark. "Nice reflexes," Xavier remarked, pushing the barrel down until it pointed at the ground.

"Thanks," she acknowledged, hand trembling. "I told you I was a trained guide."

Two men walked into the clearing, moving shadows in the light of the moon.

"So you did," Xavier conceded. Moving past her, he wrapped an arm around one man, then the other and walked them over to Bethany. They wore black, as well. "This is Sebastian." Xavier pushed one man forward. As tall as Xavier, his lean physique and short hair made her think of a swimmer.

"And Tomas." An inch shorter than Xavier, Tomas was broad and radiated a quiet strength. He shrugged Xavier off. "Good evening, Bethany. We're pleased to meet you."

"Xavier has told us much about you," Sebastian said, emphasizing the *much.*

Bethany snuck a glance at Xavier. He talked about her? "Like what?" she asked, curious.

"Shut up, Sebastian," Xavier growled.

"He told us how much he thinks of you," Sebastian continued, behaving as if Xavier didn't exist. "Not many women would have the *pelotas* to take on FARC, and he admires that."

"*Pelotas?*" Bethany repeated.

"It means crazy," Xavier translated, frowning. "A lack of common sense."

Sebastian laughed at the explanation and slapped Xavier on the shoulder.

Liar. The boy's club reaction made her suspect it meant

something that men thought was funny and few women found amusing. She let the lie slide, knowing she wouldn't get a truthful answer, anyway. "But you admire me?"

"Sebastian's English is sketchy. He said I think of you. He didn't say what I thought."

"My English, it not sketchy," Sebastian countered. "Now Tomas, that is another matter."

Tomas shrugged. It was obvious he understood, but was a classic man of few words. Sebastian's opposite.

"Where to, *chica?*" Sebastian asked. "You have the coordinates, yes?"

Kneeling down, Bethany opened her backpack, extracting a small flashlight and a topographic map of the country. Flicking on the light, she held it in her teeth and unfolded the map until she found the square she wanted. She handed Xavier the light. "We're here?"

"Yes," Xavier replied.

So far, so good. "We need to get to here." She put a finger on the first checkpoint. It was in the jungle and partway into the Andean mountain range, elevation one thousand feet.

"How do you know that is your sister's location?" Sebastian questioned, leaning in.

"This isn't her location," Bethany said. "She's farther along. This is part way. I'll tell you the exact coordinates once we're closer, and not until, so don't bother to push it."

The men looked more amused by her snippy retort than angry. Sebastian said something to Xavier and Tomas in Spanish and the men chuckled.

Her cheeks burned. She might not understand the language but she knew when a joke was being made at her expense. "That's rude," she retorted, folding the map into smaller square.

"What?" Xavier asked.

As if he didn't know? "Talking about me in Spanish when you know I can't understand."

The men fell silent. "Our apologies," Xavier said.

Bethany took a step back in surprise. Despite the fact she had the map and was paying him, she expected an argument. After all, her calling the shots hadn't stopped him yet.

She tucked the map into her pocket. Just when she thought she had Xavier pegged, he did something unexpected. Like apologize.

She nodded. There was nothing to do but be gracious. "Apology accepted."

He turned the flashlight on Sebastian and Tomas. "Where is the camp?"

"Just inside the jungle," Sebastian relayed, heading back the way they'd emerged.

"We're not leaving?" Bethany observed.

"Driving in the jungle during the day is difficult," Xavier explained. "At night, it is much too dangerous, even with a jeep."

She knew it wasn't wise. Even a wasteland like the desert held its dangers. But the thought of losing time, when she was so close to Samantha, made her anxious. "If we went to the starting point, we could start first thing in the morning. Maybe even hike in a kilometer or two," Bethany argued. That initial headway was easier to take than the thought of sleeping at the edge of the jungle, waiting.

"Bad idea," Xavier countered. "Night is when the predators come out, and I do not want to hit one. As far as hiking?" He let the thought drag out.

"There aren't just the larger animals, like panthers, jaguars, to worry about. There are smaller ones. Bugs that can make you sick if you touch them. Even kill you. One wrong hand placement and this rescue expedition would end."

"Look," Tomas revealed, rolling up his sleeve to his elbow.

Bethany leaned in to get a better look in the moonlight. A thick scar, the size of a silver dollar marred his forearm. "What happened?"

"I leaned against a tree."

"A tree did that?" Bethany stared in horrid fascination.

"No, an insect on the tree did that," Tomas described, unrolling his sleeve and buttoning it around his wrist. "It laid eggs in my flesh, and I had to cut them out before they hatched."

Bethany swallowed so the bile in her stomach would stay there. She'd seen some dangerous animals while working in southern Utah. Scorpions. Rattlers. Rabid coyotes. But nothing that creepy.

As much as she wanted to prove her skills to Xavier, part of being a good tracker was listening to people who knew more. And these men knew more, no argument there. "Okay, we leave at sunrise."

Eyes open, Bethany gave up trying to stay asleep. Instead, she stared in the dark that would soon disappear. She shared a tent with Xavier; Tomas and Sebastian slept in a tent adjacent to theirs. Xavier lay inches away from her, his breathing even in sleep.

Soon, it would be time to get up and begin their trek. She'd been so eager to get moving, but now that she was lying in the dark, stuck in her head, trepidation set in.

She'd told Xavier she knew where Samantha was located, and said it with confidence that eluded her now. What if one of the ex-hostages remembered wrong? What if she miscalculated the timing of moving between camps? What if Cesar wasn't as predictable as she thought?

She rested her head on her forearm, her hand touching the backpack that Sebastian had prepared for her. She'd glanced in it before they'd turned in. It held the traditional items. Flares. Bug spray. Water bottle.

It also held nontraditional items. Ammunition. Climbing harness. An earpiece. And camouflage paint.

Somehow, the unfamiliar items seemed to solidify her mission. Made it more real. And that raised the doubts that plagued her now. Made her question her information. After all, one wrong move and she wouldn't find Samantha. And might harm Eva's chance at freedom.

She turned over again, not bothering to cover her sigh. She prayed it would be light soon. Under most circumstances, she liked the night. She enjoyed spending time in her head, exploring her thoughts and motivations.

This was not one of those times. There was too much she wanted, *needed,* to ignore. In the tent next to theirs, one of the other men started to snore, drowning out the jungle sounds.

"Worried?" Xavier whispered.

Bethany stiffened. She'd thought he was asleep. "A little," she admitted. "I've never been in the jungle."

"Ask when you are unsure. You are a desert person. There will be dangers here that you don't know."

Calming her racing heart, she faced him in the dark. "I know. Panthers and bugs."

"And FARC," he added.

"As if I could forget," she said. "As if either of us could."

The rustle of cloth told her that he was turning over. "You know nature. You don't know men. Not like this," he stressed, his voice came at her. "It is not too late to change your mind."

Her smiled faded. "Why do you keep pressing the issue?" she protested. "You know what I'll say. Why bother?"

For a long beat, there was nothing but silence. Was he worried she'd be hurt? Or that she'd screw up? Where was his concern, for her or for the hostages?

"There are many reasons," he replied, offering nothing in the way of satisfaction. "But I keep hoping you will come to your senses before it is too late."

Bethany bit her lip. Though it was foolish, a little part of her had hoped for a more intimate answer.

She felt like a fool. A pathetic, needy fool.

She could take the guilt and the lies but she drew the line at weak. "No one ever said I was sensible," she said. "That's Samantha."

"Ah, she is the smart one, and you are the one with the with *pelotas grandes.*"

Bethany shifted again and realized Xavier was no longer a shadow in a shadow. Daylight had arrived. Finally. "What does that really mean?" she asked.

"What does what mean?" he asked. "Smart? If you have to ask, then you are not."

He teased. It was a nice and needed change from the thoughts that plagued her, refusing her even a good night's sleep. She smacked him on the shoulder. "*Pelotas.* What does it mean?"

"It means, uh." He flipped open his sleeping bag, cupped his hand and held it level with his crotch. "*Pelotas.* You know."

"Balls?" she asked. "You're saying I have big balls."

His eyes widened, as if realizing what he'd just said. He bolted upright and then ducked his head, but not before she saw the red tint to his face. "We should break camp and go."

Bethany stared at his back as he fumbled to get up and away from her. Who would have guessed that saying a word like "balls" would embarrass Xavier Monero?

"Xavier? What's wrong?" she joked, tapping him on the shoulder to try and make him face her. She knew it was mean and childish, but the urge was impossible to resist.

"Be quick," he muttered as he unzipped the tent and stepped outside.

Bethany thumped the sleeping bag with her heels. "I win," she stated, grinning.

Chapter 4

"Careful," Xavier warned as he grabbed Bethany's wrist when she reached out to push a broad, deep-green leaf out of her way. Her eyes followed a path from where he gripped her to the leaf.

It seemed safe enough, until a spot of pale green and lavender moved. She squinted and a tree frog came into view. Half the length of her pinky, its tiny suctioned feet gripped the leaf, keeping it fixed in place.

"Cute," she remarked. "And can kill me with a single touch?"

"Yes," Xavier answered.

"Thanks," she added, shaking Xavier's grip and giving the leaf a wide berth.

"You have to be more careful," Xavier urged, following her with Sebastian and then Tomas trailing. "One wrong move and you won't be hurt, you'll be dead."

She waved off the warning with a glibness she didn't feel.

She'd rotated into the point position earlier, eager to cover ground and confident in her abilities, her strength, and that while desert knowledge wasn't applicable in the Colombian jungle, basic survival principles remained the same.

But that was two hours ago and between the ache in her biceps and shoulder that came from swinging the machete and now what she'd forever call "the tiny frog incident," her confidence was waning.

She hacked at a thick vine and the machete stuck halfway. Her shoulders slumped, and it took all her strength to not drop to her knees in defeat.

Her words from yesterday echoed in her head. *You can set me in the middle of nowhere—jungle or desert—with nothing but a knife and the clothes on my back, I'll walk out of there alive.*

Well, she'd live as long as she avoided frogs. That much was true.

But she hated the jungle more and more with each step. "Stupid vines," she muttered, working to free the blade.

The desert was just as tough and demanding, but she knew the desert. The heat of the sun on her shoulders. The wind over her ears. The sense that one could walk forever and see nothing but pale sand and red rock.

The jungle was the opposite. Leaves pressed in, making her claustrophobic. Water dripped, leaving nothing untouched. And the noise never ended. Grunts. Squeals. Screeches. She missed the silence.

Plus, there were bugs here. She thought they wouldn't be a big deal, but they were everywhere. They ate the leaves, scurried across the ground and flew through the air. A millipede caught her attention as it dashed up a tree trunk. Bethany shuddered. Damn, she hated bugs.

At least the heat was familiar. She stumbled as the blade came free, caught herself and took a deep breath to regain her composure. It wouldn't do to have the men think her weak or whiny. "Onward," she said, pointing forward with the tip of the machete's blade.

"In a minute," Xavier declared. "It's time to switch off."

Oh, thank God. Despite her relief, she forced herself to smile and give the illusion that she was as tough as she claimed. "I can keep going. I don't mind," she fibbed.

Xavier held out his hand. She gave him the machete, took a step back and surveyed him. His clothes were just as damp and she knew he was tired, but he looked at home in the jungle. As if he was in his natural element.

Bethany wiped her forehead with the hem of her shirt and wished she found beauty in the green. Maybe one day. But until Samantha was free, it was hard to see the jungle as anything other than her sister's prison.

"Tomas." Xavier held up the blade. The shorter man pushed forward from the back of the small group, took the machete and began cutting a swath through the vines and leaves with an ease that Bethany envied.

Bethany let Sebastian move past her, took a spot in the middle and forced herself to keep the pace Tomas set.

"You are doing much better than I expected," Xavier remarked, from behind her.

"Thanks," she replied, surprised by the compliment. If he gave an inch, so could she. "It's harder than I expected."

"We will take a break soon," Xavier indicated.

"Don't take one on account of me," she said, then realized how defensive she sounded, but she couldn't take it back, either.

He chuckled.

Her cheeks burned.

"It's almost noon," Xavier continued. "We break for lunch and everyone needs to change their socks."

"Change socks?" Bethany asked.

"Yes," Xavier confirmed. "Boots and damp socks are a bad

combination. We might be here for a few days, but in the jungle, it only takes a few hours for the skin to become saturated with water. Once that happens, any wound can become infected and from there, gangrene."

"Ew."

"That is my point. We dry our feet, put on fresh socks and then continue."

She wiggled her toes inside her shoes. The thought of mold growing on her feet made her want to stop now. A rustle behind them caught her attention. She glanced over her shoulder, her senses pricked by the unexpected sound. "Xavier?"

"I heard it, too," he disclosed, his brows pressed together.

There was another rustle—closer now—then the distinct sound of leaves being trod. Shivers raced up Bethany's arms.

Xavier's eyes narrowed. "Tell the others to keep walking. Act normal." He dropped back then off the trail.

Act normal? When they were being stalked? Bethany hurried forward as fast as she dared without attracting attention. "Sebastian, we're being followed," she informed him. "Xavier is checking it out. Keep moving."

Sebastian unclipped the strap over his gun and they moved onward with Tomas keeping point.

Bethany lagged a few steps, straining to listen. Was it FARC? She couldn't imagine they'd trailed the group. They'd either shoot them or in a more probable scenario, take them all hostage.

So their shadow wasn't human. But whatever followed them was large. A monkey perhaps? Jaguar?

The thought of a big cat tracking them made her shudder but better a big cat than FARC. The cat was more forgiving. She looked up and realized that Sebastian and Tomas were almost out of sight. Not that disappearing in the jungle was difficult. All it took was a few seconds of inattention.

She increased her pace and the leaves next to her moved.

Bethany slowed. "Xavier?" she whispered. There was no answer. Her mouth went dry.

"Here, kitty, kitty, kitty," she croaked, half teasing and hoping like hell she was wrong.

A low growl replied.

The hairs on the back of Bethany's neck rose in response. "Oh, crap." She swallowed the sudden panic and forced her feet to move faster and close the space between her and the men.

"Sebastian?" She tried to call his name but her voice came out a whisper.

The growl was ahead of her now, just off to the right and between her and the rest of the team. She stopped. Her breath came in staccato gasps. Why was a jaguar hunting during the day? They were nocturnal creatures. The only explanation was that this cat was either sick or hurt, which also meant reckless, out of its head and twice as dangerous.

Still rooted to the spot, she looked over her shoulder. "Xavier?" she whispered again. He didn't answer.

Was he lost? He was in his element but even professionals got lost. She'd seen guides get disoriented in the desert even when the sky was visible for navigation.

The jungle, with its canopy and mass of green, had to be worse. The thought of Xavier wandering the jungle was almost as stressful as the thought of fending off a cat that weighed as much as her. "Xavier?" Still no answer.

Her mouth went dry. It was up to her to escape the situation. She put one foot in front of the other. Just a few steps, she told herself. A few steps and she'd be past the cat. And once she caught up to the others, she'd be safe with the group.

One. She forced her right foot forward.

Two. Left foot.

Three. Right. She was even with the big cat now, but she kept her focus on her feet, afraid that if she made eye contact with the creature, she'd either break into a run or wet herself.

Neither seemed like a good idea. The scent of the beast wafted over her, thick and with a putrid overlay. It was wounded. Cats never smelled. Not like that.

Four. Left foot. She passed the cat and still, it remained in the bushes.

Five. Bethany laid a hand on her chest in relief. She wasn't safe, but if it hadn't attacked now, she might, just might, get away with her skin intact.

The rustling next to her grew louder and the shadow paralleled her movements. The cat was tracking her again.

Then it moved forward, ahead of her.

Not tracking, she realized.

Keeping her separated.

Xavier crouched low and peered through the leaves. The bone thin jaguar he'd been trailing crouched three feet from Bethany. An open wound on its side oozed blood and pus.

He looked past her. Tomas and Sebastian were out of sight, lost among the leaves. Once Bethany was safe, he'd have their heads for this carelessness. He'd also have a word with Bethany for allowing herself to become separated.

But right now, there were bigger issues.

Like keeping the pretty *desert* guide alive.

A flicker of movement caught his attention. Bethany took a step back. The cat took a step forward.

She shifted her left foot, as if ready to sprint into motion away from the beast. His breath caught. It would have her in its claws before she got three feet away.

Don't run, Bethany. Don't even breathe.

Bethany froze.

Good. He took a breath. The skill she placed so much importance in seemed to kick in, overriding the flight mode. Her eyes locked on the big cat, she slid her hand down and unsnapped the leather strap to the gun on her right hip.

He'd considered the idea himself, but one shot and everyone within a ten-mile radius would know they were here.

That scenario would be less than useful considering this was a secret mission. And despite her bravado and bragging, he'd never seen her fire a weapon. If she missed, she'd make the cat angry, and angry cats were unpredictable and more dangerous.

The mere thought of her being mauled made every muscle in his body tense with unwelcome anticipation.

Mine. The primal part of his brain screamed possession. She was his to care for. His to help.

And he protected what was his.

Xavier moved through the jungle, as silent as the cat he'd shadowed, then stepped onto the trail next to Bethany.

She jumped but held ground.

Ahead of them, the jaguar hissed, raised a foot and batted the air. It didn't run. Damn. He'd hoped that sufficient opposition would persuade it to go after easier game.

"I leave you for two minutes and you get into trouble," Xavier said, pulling his weapon while keeping his attention on the cat.

"You call this trouble?" Bethany slid her hand into his. "I'm not the one who got lost."

"You were worried? Nice to know you care." He squeezed her fingers. He knew it might be South American machismo but now that he stood next to her, he knew everything would be okay. He could protect her. Keep her safe.

"You wish," she corrected, keeping her voice low, and nodding toward the big cat. "I've always told my clients to make themselves look bigger. Make noise. Want to test that theory?"

He didn't want to kill the jaguar. Not unless there was no choice. "One. Two."

On three, they raised their arms over their heads. Shouting, they stamped their feet and ran two steps toward the cat.

Its slitted eyes narrowed, the jaguar snarled at the pair, and for a blip in time, Xavier wasn't sure what it would do.

Xavier lunged forward another half step. The cat hissed then ran into the jungle, its spotted coat blending with the foliage.

That was close. Too close. Still holding Bethany's hand, he lowered their arms. Sliding his weapon back into its holster, Xavier pulled her to his chest, relief flooding him.

For a brief moment, there was no Sebastian. No Tomas. No jaguar. There was only Bethany and the need to celebrate cheating death.

"Wow," Bethany said, laughter in her voice. She looked up at him, her green eyes bright, her cheeks flushed and her lips parted. He wanted to kiss her. Again.

"*Ese,* that was intense." Sebastian and Tomas came toward them. "We saw the whole thing."

Xavier pushed Bethany away. "Where the hell were you?" he growled. Every terrifying scenario he'd repressed while dealing with the situation surged forward. "It's your job to guard her."

Sebastian's unending, easy smile turned into a frown. "Did you think we'd let her be turned into cat food? Once we realized she'd lagged behind, we came back, but the cat was between us."

"She was never in any real danger," Tomas added.

"Xavier." Bethany touched his arm. "I'm fine. We're fine. Let's not make an issue of it."

Xavier looked back at her. Her cheeks were still flushed.

"I'm a little shaken," Bethany admitted, "but no one was hurt so I call it a successful encounter."

Xavier wasn't so sure. He'd never been that close to a big cat. It was thrilling, humbling and he never wanted to do it again— especially not with Bethany next to him. Seeing her in danger shook him more than he expected, and he didn't like surprises.

"We still have light. Isn't it a little early to stop?" Bethany asked. Nightfall was over an hour away and they'd been making good time with the adrenaline from the jaguar encounter to spur them.

She wanted to get as far as possible. Hell, given a choice, she'd use a flashlight and hike through the night.

Though she couldn't imagine the men agreeing and even she knew it wasn't a great idea. Being cornered by a jaguar was frightening during the day, but the thought of being stalked by one at night made her shudder and rethink her place in the food chain. She might as well roll around in a marinade and write "eat me" on her forehead.

"A little," Xavier agreed. Sliding his pack off his shoulders, he lowered it to the ground and bent to unbuckle the straps.

In the brush behind them, Bethany caught a glimpse of Sebastian and Tomas as they scouted for any obvious dangers and set a few traps.

Xavier continued, "But this is a good location, and we can't count on finding another one."

"What's so good?" Bethany prodded, offering a guide's curiosity about her new jungle environment as she set her pack next to Xavier's. "Why here instead of under the trees?" They stood in a clearing, free from the canopy for the first time since they had begun their hike into the jungle.

"You noticed?" he asked sounding surprised.

He didn't expect much from her, did he? She might be a desert guide, but it didn't limit her observation skills to the Mohave. "I can see the sky. Of course I noticed," she replied, keeping her tone as professional as possible.

Until now, the jungle world obliterated the blue above them, allowing only the occasional shaft of light to break the leafy monotony. "Aren't we more sheltered there?" Her back to him, she bent down to pull out her gear for the night. Now that the adrenaline waned, sleep sounded perfect.

"We are," he agreed. The leaves on the ground crunched as he came up behind her. "But shelter isn't everything. Turn around."

"Excuse me?" Bethany looked up at him, shielding her eyes from the sun with an open palm.

"Stand up and turn around."

What did he want? A fight? To talk?

Another kiss?

The thought made her shiver but she rose. "What?"

Xavier placed his hands on her shoulders, and for a moment, Bethany stiffened.

"Relax. Shut your eyes."

"Why?"

"Humor me."

Humor him? Lips pursed, she considered the request. "I suppose you earned it," she mused. After all, he had saved her from the jaguar.

He rolled his eyes and turned her away from him. "Shut your eyes," he whispered in her ear.

A shiver rushed from the base of Bethany's spine to her shoulders, and the sudden sense of cotton in her mouth had nothing to do with fear.

She shut her eyes.

Xavier leaned closer, until her back was pressed against his chest.

"Imagine the jungle at night," he elaborated, surprising her with a whisper, his voice as warm as his breath against the side of her bare neck.

"See the dark sky. No moon. Just stars and the fire on the ground, illuminating the night."

She pictured it in her mind, and it was just as beautiful as the desert. His hands slid down her arms, leaving heat in their wake. "Do you see it?"

Bethany nodded, hypnotized by his voice, the vision he created and his touch.

His hands slid back up her arms. "Now, see this as if from a distance. See the fire under the trees. The shadows it creates. The flickering of the flames."

Bethany translated the scene to the desert. Taking shelter

beneath a rock shelf—not the canopy but the same effect. In her mind, she watched herself lighting a fire and the light reflected off the rock, just as it would reflect off the canopy. Both stone and leaf would glow with the flame.

And announce their presence to anyone within a few miles. "The reflection on the canopy gives us away," she murmured.

Xavier's hands tightened on her shoulders and he turned her back to face him.

Bethany opened her eyes, not sure what to expect. Sometimes Xavier seemed to expect nothing from her. Sometimes, he seemed to expect everything.

What greeted her was curiosity and pleasure. "Yes."

She wanted more of that look, and the ribbon of warmth that followed caught her off guard. To want anything from Xavier was asking for trouble. But to want his approval?

She was safer with the jaguar.

"Why are you looking at me like that?" she asked, fighting back the sense of warmth. She didn't want that feeling. Not in association with him.

He tucked a strand of hair behind her ear, unaffected by the challenge in her voice. "You really are a guide, aren't you?"

"Did you think it was just talk?"

He shrugged. "It crossed my mind. This is your sister. A lie or two would not be out of line in getting what you want."

A lie or two? Did he know about the money? The ribbon of warmth chilled. Did he already know?

She swallowed back the rush of fear. He couldn't know. If he did, she wouldn't be here and he wouldn't be risking Eva's freedom for a stranger with no cash.

She forced herself to smile up at him. "I don't have to lie," she replied. "I'm a helluva guide."

For a moment, he stared into her eyes then he cupped her jaw with his hands. "I believe you."

Chapter 5

Xavier came out of the jungle, his hands empty. "Nothing in the snares," he informed.

Taking a seat next to Bethany, he picked up his plate of rice and refried black beans. "Who taught you two how to set a trap?" he asked, gesturing with his fork.

"You," Sebastian replied.

Bethany snickered then shifted her focus to her plate when Xavier flashed a scowl at her.

"Bethany and I will take first watch. We sleep two to a tent tonight," he announced.

Bethany's fork stopped midway to her mouth. She'd been fighting the ghost of his touch since he left to go check the perimeter, and the thought of sleeping next to him unsettled her. "I'm sleeping with you?"

"Two to a tent."

"Why?"

"Jaguars," he answered. "Or rather one jaguar, in particular."

"Did you see it?"

He shook his head as he finished a mouthful of food. "No, but I found fresh tracks. It's wary of the group, but it's out there, waiting for one of us to break away from the pack, as it were.

"Besides," Xavier continued, "we slept in the same tent last night. What's the problem now?"

"Has something changed, *chica?*" Sebastian asked, his tone teasing. "Tomas can take the shift if you like, and you can sleep with me."

He wished. Bethany set her plate down. "Nothing's changed."

She'd deal. After all, this was her issue. Obviously, it didn't bother Xavier. At all. Which made her angrier. "It's *fine*," she snapped. "Just fine."

Xavier turned to her, his face shadowed in the light. "I wasn't asking your approval," he asserted, his voice tight.

Bethany glared at him, annoyed that he remained so unaffected. But the better question was, why did it bother her?

Taking a deep breath, she let the anger leave with the exhale. "I wasn't giving approval. I was commenting, as a professional, that it was a good idea."

"And I am saying—"

"Do we need to get you two a room?" Sebastian interrupted.

Bethany whipped her head around to glare at the man. "Excuse me?"

"All this tension. Fighting. *Passion.* You two are either going to kill each other or make love. I'm betting on the latter, though Tomas says differently."

Bethany's eyes widened. "Excuse me? That is out of line." She turned to Xavier, but his arched eyebrows told her that he was just as surprised by Sebastian's outburst.

"Leave me out of this," Tomas muttered. Rising, he stretched, muscular arms high over his head. "I am going to bed."

"*Ese,* I'm just teasing them," Sebastian called as Tomas walked to the tent.

"Now isn't the time," Xavier reminded. "Get some rest. We leave at daybreak."

"You're the boss. You two work this out. *Buenas noches.*"

Sebastian put his plate down and went to his tent, leaving them alone.

Bethany pushed her food around with her spoon, but the rice and black beans no longer looked appetizing. She glanced at Xavier through her lashes. He devoured the rest of his dinner.

She envied his ability to shrug it all away.

"Even if you're not hungry, you should eat," Xavier commented. "You'll be grateful for the calories tomorrow."

She hated it when he was right. Picking up a spoonful, she forced herself to chew and swallow.

"Don't let Sebastian get to you," Xavier reflected, setting his plate on the ground. "He talks a lot. Almost as much as a woman."

Bethany's fork dropped to her tin plate, the ping like a fighter's bell.

Then she noticed the smile in Xavier's eyes. "You're teasing me, aren't you?" she guessed.

He shrugged. "You seemed upset."

Xavier was the most confusing man she'd ever met. One moment he acted annoyed with her. The next, he teased her with a familiarity that touched her. As if they knew each other. Which they didn't. She shook her head, puzzled.

"You weren't upset?" he asked.

She shook her head again. "I was, but—" She stopped herself, not sure how much she wanted to reveal. Despite their shared troubles with FARC, she and Xavier were strangers.

"But what?" Xavier pressed

"You confuse me," she confessed before her brain caught up with her sense of emotional preservation and told her to shut the hell up.

His grin broadened. "*I* confuse *you?*"

"You do."

"How so?" His curiosity seemed genuine.

Bethany opened her mouth and then clamped it shut. She didn't want to have this conversation. It was too much. Too close. She had enough drama to concern her without adding more.

Besides, he didn't want her on the rescue mission. He'd tried to talk her out of coming.

What if his curiosity was another manipulation? It was hard to tell. As much as she wanted to confide in someone, it couldn't be Xavier. She'd seen the charm. Felt the *woo*.

And it left her confused and wanting.

"You just do," she finished, her reply sounding lame even to her own ears.

Xavier shrugged again, but she noticed the disappointment in his eyes. "Time to pay attention," he declared. Taking out his guns, he took the safeties off and set them on his lap.

Bethany followed suit.

Ten minutes later, she wished he'd say something. Anything. It wasn't as if the jungle was silent. Bugs chirped. The occasional breeze rustled the leaves on the tree. And unknown animal noises punctuated the quieter sounds.

But the silence between her and Xavier was louder than anything else, as far as Bethany was concerned.

Bethany adjusted her position, stretching her legs out then crossing them in front of her. She glanced at Xavier. He sat as still as a rock. She envied that.

Little flickers of light in the jungle caught her attention. Cocking her gun, she squinted for a better view. "What are those?" She'd read about them but never expected they'd light up the dark like crazy, hypnotic Christmas lights.

"You've never seen them?"

"We don't have fireflies in the desert," she said her voice low. She was unable to look away. "They're beautiful."

"I thought you hated bugs," Xavier contradicted.

I do," she said. "But not all. Just the ones that lay eggs in people's arms."

She remembered how she would hunt for caterpillars when she was young. She'd kept them, feeding them and waiting for the moment when they cocooned and morphed into butterflies. She hated creepy, crawly bugs but these little spots of brightness, she could deal with these.

On the other hand, Samantha thought bugs, all bugs, were cool. "Samantha would love this," she reminisced, her chest tightening.

Xavier looked over at her. "She's okay, you know."

Just when she'd convinced herself the mercenary didn't care about her, he saw past her words and into the meaning.

Jerk.

A tear slipped down her cheek. Damn, she hated crying, and that was all she seemed to do as of late. She brushed it away. "I know." Her voice broke and she took a deep breath, forcing herself to remain calm. "They'll keep her alive. But is she hurt? Is she hungry? I hate not knowing."

Xavier slid closer, until they were thigh to thigh. Running his hand up her back, he guided her head to his shoulder and stroked her hair.

Bethany sighed. Unlike his earlier heated caress, this one was comforting. Safe. And right now, she needed safe. She needed to feel like everything was going to be all right.

"Tell me about Samantha," he ventured.

Tell him about Samantha? Bethany smiled. "My sister was the kid who brought home hurt animals. Spoke to the new kid in school. She's always been the one who watched out for those weaker. She's the good one." She thought about the last time she and Samantha were together. The teasing and taunting and how her sister had refused to retaliate. "The nicer one."

Xavier chuckled, his laugh low and comforting. "You are not so bad."

Bethany wiped away the last of the tears. "Gee. Thanks."

"I do what I can." He stroked her hair again. "Tell me more," he said.

"What do you want to know?" Bethany asked, eyes still open, watching the lights.

"Your best memory," he whispered.

She sighed at the suggestion. There was no best memory of her and Samantha. Just Bethany, being bitchy.

"The last Christmas we were together," she lied. "When she told me about the contracting job that brought her to Colombia."

When she'd shot her sister down. Ridiculed her.

"I was so proud of Samantha. So pleased she got the job. It was an adventure."

I wanted it for myself. I was jealous. Cruel.

"I've never been more proud of her."

I wanted to show her up.

"You love her very much," Xavier remarked, still stroking her hair.

"More than anything," Bethany replied.

That much was true.

The pain that consumed Bethany was almost as tangible as the jungle that surrounded them, and Xavier found himself unable to resist touching her. But not as a lover, he told himself as he stroked her hair, tracing the pattern of the braid. This was comfort. Nothing more.

Liar.

She sniffled and a tear slid down her cheek before she swiped it away with an angry fist. "Sorry. It's just that, Christmas was the last time I saw her."

"It's okay," he responded. These tears he understood. He still didn't like them, but he understood.

"Tell me about you," she encouraged.

"Me?" The thought of revealing himself made him more uncomfortable than tears.

"You," she coaxed, poking him in the chest with her free hand. "Tell me about you and Eva."

"There's not much to tell," he stated.

"Not good enough." She sat up, her cheeks pink from crying. "How about growing up? Did she tag along after you? Did you get along?"

"Yes," he agreed. Eva had followed because she had no choice. He was her brother. Her protector.

"And your parents? How are they taking all this?" she pressed.

"They died when I was ten," Xavier disclosed. "Car accident."

Bethany's hand touched his arm. "I'm sorry."

"Don't be. It was a long time ago." He'd told the story so many times it seemed to belong to someone else. Something he related to with total emotional detachment.

Except that he wasn't detached. Not really. But the pretense made the pain bearable and allowed him to be the man that others needed him to be. That Bethany needed him to be.

Bethany's hand grasped his, and she squeezed hard. "I lost my Dad when I was sixteen, and it almost tore our family apart. I can't imagine losing both parents. And at the same time."

Xavier stared past her into the small fire. He'd never forget the day his parents died. The police at the door. His siblings' tears. His tears.

He hadn't shed one since. Not even when Miguel died.

"What happened after they died?" Bethany asked. "Where did you go?"

"The streets."

Bethany eyes widened. "Excuse me?"

Xavier's cheeks heated with embarrassment. He hadn't

meant to reveal so much, but there was something about the night and the fire—about Bethany—that made him careless.

He'd have to be more careful in the future.

Still, now that he'd opened his mouth, it was a little late to take it back. She wasn't the type to let things go.

He knew that all too well.

Besides, information about his childhood wasn't secret. There was nothing there of importance. Just memories, he told himself. "There was no one to take us in. No family that wanted us. So we went to the streets."

"It must have been difficult."

He nodded. They'd begged. Eaten garbage scraps. Slept huddled together under bits of cloth they'd used to make a blanket of sorts. "It wasn't easy, but it could have been worse."

There were children who had sold themselves for money. Men had made offers for Eva—hell, they'd made offers for him and Miguel—but he'd promised himself and his siblings that they would never do that.

He'd seen the empty eyes of enough child prostitutes to know that they'd sold more than their bodies. They'd sold their souls.

Not that most were offered a choice in their profession. Pimps preyed on them, and they were easy targets. Hunger, sickness, desperation and fear were the men's tools. He remembered one pimp, *El Lagarto*.

A thug who used his fists to intimidate, he would force children to sell their bodies. When that wasn't effective, he had used drugs and addiction to demand compliance.

Xavier and his siblings avoided the pimps by stealth and by watching out for each other. That simple commitment to each other had kept them alive and strong, even in the worst of times.

"Tell me more," Bethany insisted. "Tell me about Miguel. What was he like?"

Xavier hesitated. He hadn't spoken of Miguel to anyone but

Eva in a very long time, but with Bethany, it felt right. "Miguel was the funny one of our little trio. He did silly tumbling acts and told jokes to make Eva smile. Comedy was his weapon of choice. Even when life was at its lowest." He smiled, thinking of his brother's many fake falls and how Eva would giggle every time.

She loved physical humor.

"And Eva?"

He stared into the fire, missing her. "A good laugh. Tough. Wants to change the world."

"Like you," Bethany affirmed.

Xavier froze. Change the world? He'd already tried that, and while he hadn't failed, it wasn't something he wanted to be a part of. Not anymore. He'd sacrificed his brother. And now, his sister. He picked up a stick and tossed it on the fire. "I am a bartender. That is all."

"And a rebel leader," Bethany added. "Someone who rescues people from FARC."

She made him sound like a hero. Her admiration warmed him more than the flames and made him want to lay her down in the firelight and make love to her.

To be the man she saw.

But he wasn't that man. Not anymore. And they'd both do well to remember that. "I do those things for a price," Xavier reminded her. "For no other reason. Do not romanticize me."

"The fee. I'd almost forgotten that," Bethany said.

He thought of Eva and Miguel. All the friends and family he'd lost by being the hero. "I didn't."

"Wake up."

Bethany jerked upright, embarrassed to have fallen asleep on watch. "I'm not asleep. I was resting my—"

He put a finger to her lips, shushing her. The cock of his head and tension of his posture told her that he didn't shush her for convenience.

There was danger. And it was close.

She'd beat herself up later. She nodded, showing she understood the situation.

He leaned in until his mouth touched the rim of her ear. "We have another cat. Maybe the one from earlier. Maybe not."

"Did you see it?"

He pointed toward the jungle.

She followed his line of vision. Glowing eyes stared at them. Bethany swallowed hard. "This must be what a mouse feels like." There were few thoughts more horrifying than being dragged off by a jaguar.

Xavier took a stick from the fire and rose. "What the hell do you think you're doing?" Bethany asked in a stage whisper. "The fire is the one thing keeping us safe."

He looked at her then out into the darkness. "I'll only be a minute."

Men. Why did they have to act like heroes? "What are you going to do? Wrestle it?"

"Scare it away."

"By yourself?" She rose and pulled another branch from the fire. "Two are better than one."

He reached over and tried to take her torch, but she tightened her grip, knowing he couldn't fight too hard for control without putting both of them at risk for a nasty burn.

He pulled harder. She dug in her feet and pulled back.

A low growl rolled through the camp. Both froze. "All this movement is making it angry," Xavier whispered.

"I go or neither of us goes," Bethany implored. She pulled harder. "Now let go."

He released the stick with a sigh of exasperation. "You are difficult and a pain in my ass."

"Ditto."

His lips pressed together in a tight frown as he peered at the predator. "We need to know if it's the wounded cat. I will go check the situation. You will stay and guard Sebastian and Tomas."

Bethany rubbed the back of her neck. He spoke as if there was no argument, as if they hadn't just played tug-of-war seconds ago.

As if what she said made no difference.

She glanced at her watch. One hand on the twelve with the other on six. Thirty minutes to shift change. Close enough.

Keeping her focus on the glowing eyes, Bethany pushed past Xavier and went to the tent.

"What are you doing?" Xavier hissed.

Unzipping the tent, she was greeted with the wrong end of Tomas's gun. Sebastian continued to snore.

"The cat is back," Bethany whispered.

Tomas tapped on Sebastian's forehead with the butt end of his weapon. "Get up."

"Xavier and I will check it out," Bethany insisted. "Move slow. It's close."

She stepped back out and faced Xavier, one hand on her hip. "Problem solved."

Seconds later, both Tomas and Sebastian emerged carrying their guns and wearing nothing but T-shirts, boxers and socks.

"*¿Qué pasa?*" Sebastian whispered.

Xavier pointed toward the jungle. The glowing eyes were no longer visible, but the hairs on Bethany's neck rose. It was still out there. She didn't doubt that.

"*Gato grande,*" Xavier answered.

Sebastian took the safety off his weapon. "Don't get eaten."

Xavier tossed his branch back into the fire and pulled a flashlight from his pocket. "Keep yours," he instructed. "It might help us scare the cat away."

He turned on his heel and Bethany followed. Unholstering

one of her weapons, she held the pistol in one hand and the torch in the other. Xavier might demand secrecy but that wouldn't matter if he were dead.

The darkness closed in around them, making Bethany's torch seem minute and unimportant. "This was a bad idea," she murmured.

Xavier didn't answer. A branch cracked under her feet, and she cringed at the snap. Then again, she was walking through the jungle carrying a flaming stick. Did noise even matter at this point? It might scare the cat away, though if it were the one from earlier, there was no way to be certain.

Xavier stopped, bent down and pushed the debris aside. There was a paw print. Fresh. Feline. She shook her head. She was a good guide and tracker, but Xavier's tracking skills were exceptional. There was no doubt about that.

They headed in the direction the paw angled. She nodded and let him continue to lead. Ten more feet and he pointed out a leaf. A darkness stained it. She stopped and touched it with her finger, smearing it across the leaf.

Blood.

It was their wounded jaguar.

Great.

A low growl sounded again. Once again, Bethany's heart slammed against her chest and every cell in her body screamed *run*.

Then Xavier's hand was in hers. The internal screaming stopped, leaving a calm strength in its wake. Xavier looked at her, their faces illuminated with his flashlight.

Okay? he mouthed.

She nodded. This was a bad idea.

He nodded back. Letting go of her, he pulled his weapon out and motioned for Bethany to return the way they'd come. The growling grew louder.

Seconds later, Bethany spotted the cat. Crouched low, with

its hindquarters up in the air and tail lashing, it appeared poised to attack.

She unlocked the safety on her weapon. Screw him being a hero. And screw being quiet.

The cat froze.

Seconds later, the distinct sounds of men crashing through the jungle interrupted the growling and large lights washed over them. The cat bolted.

Xavier grabbed the makeshift torch from her hand and ground it under his shoe as he pulled her to the ground. "Hunters!"

Saviors were more like it. Relief as strong as adrenaline rushed through her, and she covered her head with her hands, keeping low.

Shouts of anger and excitement sounded around them. More gunshots. Men raced past them.

Then two sets of black-booted feet stopped next in front of her. *"¿Cómo te llamas?"* A deep voice demanded.

Bethany uncovered her head, following the boots upward to military-issue fatigues and then to the Colombian bars of ranking on the soldier's pocket. Her stomach lurched. It wasn't the cavalry that saved them.

It was the Colombian army.

In her case, they were almost as dangerous as FARC. If they discovered what she was doing, she'd be spending the rest of her quality time in a cell.

She had to make sure that didn't happen.

"Thank God you arrived," Bethany greeted, rising to her knees and looking up at the soldier towering over her and praying he believed her. "We were camping and there's a jaguar out there."

"Be quiet," Xavier whispered as more men arrived. One of the soldiers yanked Xavier's arms behind his back. "They don't care, and I don't think they understand you."

Bethany shrugged. It was a lame lie in any language.

Shouting orders in Spanish, the soldier yanked her to her feet as confirmation while two more grabbed Xavier—one on each arm.

"What do we do?" Bethany asked Xavier, as the man who found them wound her wrists with a length of rope.

"Whatever they say," Xavier said.

"They can't just take us." She tried to jerk away from the soldier.

Another soldier came through the brush, two bags in hand.

"Bethany, don't struggle," Xavier insisted. "This will be fine. I promise."

She didn't have time to respond before the bag was jammed over her head.

Chapter 6

Her hands still trussed behind her back, Bethany lay motionless on the ground until her captors left. She counted to thirty in case they came back, but nothing broke the silence.

Was Xavier even here? They'd been dragged through the jungle and she hadn't heard a word from him since.

"Xavier?" she whispered.

"Over here," he replied. "Are you okay?"

She inched toward his voice, scraping the burlap bag off her head. Blinking dust and fibers from her eyes, she realized they were in a tent.

Xavier sat ten feet away, his legs out in front of him with a lit halogen lantern on one side and his burlap bag on the other.

Rolling to her knees, she winced as her hip hit a rock, but it was no worse than the other bruises she'd gathered as the soldiers forced them to trek, blind and bound, through the nighttime jungle and then shoved them in the back of a vehicle.

All would heal in time, providing she had time. "I'm good. You?"

He nodded in response.

Still on her knees, she shuffled towards Xavier. "Where are Sebastian and Tomas?"

"They're not here," he responded. "They're smart enough to make themselves scarce and not get captured."

She didn't miss the self-recrimination and felt much the same way.

"Think they'll try to break us out?" she asked.

"There are too many soldiers," Xavier noted. "They know the rules."

She tried to hide her disappointment.

The rules were there for a reason, she told herself. And not taking on an army was a good rule. That didn't mean she liked it. "That's good." Bethany reached Xavier and plopped next to him. "Smart."

Xavier shook his head, chuckling. "Can you imagine Sebastian following a rule? Any rule?"

She smiled. "No." So help would arrive. Eventually. "What now?" she pressed. "Wait? Send up a smoke signal?"

"We free our hands," he said. Rising to his knees, they both shuffled until they were back to back. The knots were tight, but at least it was rope and not zip ties.

"Buenas noches" an unknown voice greeted.

Bethany stiffened and her hands stilled. Behind her, canvas smacked canvas as the tent flap was pushed aside and soldiers entered.

Xavier leaned back. "Stick with the hiker story," he whispered so low that it reached her ears and no farther.

Before she could respond or react, Bethany found herself hauled to her feet.

The man towering over her was new. Granted, she hadn't

seen any of the soldiers that well, but she was sure this man would have stood out.

The gray in his military-cut hair and the deep wrinkles in his forehead told her that he was pushing fifty, but the firm shoulders and toned body beneath the camouflage uniform belonged to a man decades younger.

But it was his no-nonsense attitude and the multiple bars on his pocket that told her he was the commander of the camp.

He looked her over from head to feet.

There was nothing sexual in his assessment. In fact, it felt predatory, and the hairs on Bethany's neck rose in response.

"I am Commander Franco Veron of the Colombian army." He tossed her passport to her feet.

"Bethany Darrow," she replied. She might lie about a lot, but there was no point in lying about her name when her passport told the truth.

"What are you doing in my jungle?"

Experience told her to treat him like the predator he seemed to be. Look away. Don't make eye contact. Act submissive. Instinct told her to do the opposite. And she didn't ignore instinct.

He leaned toward her, his posture daring her to step away. She didn't flinch. "I was hiking until your men kidnapped me."

"Wrong answer." He stepped back, and Bethany's knees gave as someone kicked them from behind. She fell to the ground, twisting sideways to keep from hitting her face, and whacked the side of her head instead.

Okay, her instincts were dead wrong. Dazed, she gave herself a shake, trying to clear her head.

Around her, there was shouting in Spanish. Scuffling.

She faced the source. Xavier lay a few feet from her, face down with a soldier's foot on his lower back. "Touch her again and I will make you pay," he vowed, his words muffled by the ground.

"It's okay. I'm okay," she said. God, this was worse than she realized, and she didn't see it improving.

She glared at Veron. He was supposed to be the good guy?

Groaning, she rolled onto her back. Veron took a stance over her, one foot on each side of her hips, as he stared down. Once quick move and she'd have her knee in his crotch.

The thought of Veron joining her on the ground in the kind of pain only a man could feel was a tempting thought. But stupid, she realized, as was her attempt at defiance. Veron was in charge—the quintessential alpha male of the camp.

At least until she and Xavier managed to free themselves. Then he'd find out who was stronger.

"Why are you here?" Veron's gaze intensified and she looked away, acting the submissive and hating it. "I'm a tourist," she responded. "Nothing more."

Veron held out his hand to the side, palm up. From her peripheral vision, she saw someone give him something. He dropped the object onto her chest.

The headset from her backpack.

"Why does a tourist need a military-issue headset?"

Good question. "It's the jungle," Bethany replied. "I wanted to make sure we'd find each other if I got lost." And a plausible answer.

Veron continued to stare at her, trying to unnerve her with his blank expression and daring her to confess her lie.

They were playing parts now. Alpha. Beta. Dominant. Submissive. Strong. Weak. Whatever the name, it was a role and a game, and she doubted her skill at acting like a helpless female made him trust her.

After all, he didn't command an army because he was a fool.

He held out his hand again, and a soldier gave him something new. This time, he didn't drop the item on her. He pointed it at her head. "And this?"

Bethany stared at the barrel of Xavier's SIG.

Déjà vu.

She bit her lip before she broke into hysterics.

"That's mine," Xavier interrupted, rolling onto his back. "If we didn't carry weapons in the jungle, we'd be dead. You should know that. What kind of guide would I be if I wasn't armed?"

Her guide? It was the truth in a way.

Veron's eyes narrowed as he focused his attention to Xavier. "Are you calling my intelligence into question?"

Xavier's eyes narrowed, as well. "I am pointing out the obvious, which you seem to have missed."

Veron stiffened. Stepping over Bethany, he strode the short distance to Xavier and aimed the gun at his head. "What is obvious is that you are lying," he stated, his voice as calm and indifferent as if he asked for directions. "Why does a tourist and her *guide* need a military headset and a weapon?"

Bethany's gaze slid from the gun to Xavier. He didn't blink. Didn't back away. And despite the fact that Veron was free and Xavier was bound, it wasn't clear who was winning this pissing contest.

Veron bent down, pressed the gun against Xavier's forehead and turned to face Bethany. "Well?"

She knew what he was doing. He thought her gender made her weak. That threatening Xavier would break her.

And he was right.

"Don't," she pleaded, looking up at Veron, eyes wide with fear. "Please don't."

"The truth," Veron insisted. "Now."

The truth? That would get them killed. But this was all happening too fast and she needed time to think. To plan.

Veron cocked the gun.

Time was what she didn't have. "I work with a television studio as a consultant. I'm scouting a new location for a reality show," she blurted out.

For a heartbeat, there was nothing but silence in the tent. Inside, Bethany cringed, ready for laughter, disbelief or—God forbid—a gunshot. It was a dumb lie, but the only one that came to mind as a random remnant from her job as a movie consultant.

Instead, Veron cocked his head. "Reality show?"

Hell. He didn't know what she was talking about. "You know. Like *Survivor*."

"Perdón?"

Did he never watch television? Bethany took a deep breath, willing herself to believe the lie. To put so much faith behind it that Veron had no choice but to believe. "We take a group of people, put them in an unknown, somewhat dangerous location, and then pit them against each other in a physical contest. At the end of the show, the winner gets a million dollars."

He still looked confused, but before Bethany could explain further, one of the soldiers spoke in rapid Spanish.

"Ah, *sí, sí,*" he said, nodding. "You are a location scout?"

"Yes," Bethany confirmed, a sigh of relief escaping her lips.

He looked interested, but the weapon remained pointed at Xavier. "Why claim to be a tourist?"

She shrugged. "I'm under contract to keep the location of the show a secret."

The weapon dropped an inch and now pointed at Xavier's shoulder. "What is the name of this reality show?"

Bethany's mind went blank with nothing but the name *Survivor* coming to mind.

The gun rose again to point at Xavier's head.

"Endurance," Xavier broke in. "It's called *Endurance*."

Thank God.

"Endurance?" Veron lowered the gun again.

"Yes," Bethany answered.

Veron stepped back over Xavier then walked to Bethany.

Flipping her over, he untied the rope that bound her and helped her to her feet.

She tried not to sigh in relief. Maybe they were the good guys, after all.

"We will talk more. Alone," Veron declared. "Take him away."

Or not.

"I stay with her." Xavier struggled as two soldiers tried to haul him to his feet. "She is my responsibility."

In seconds, two more soldiers were on Xavier, subduing him in a flurry of legs and fists. Bethany lurched forward before Veron grabbed her arm and yanked her to a stop.

"Stop them," she screamed, trying to pull away. "They'll kill him."

He shrugged.

She glared up at him. "You want to know more about me. The show? Hollywood?"

His eyes lit up.

Bingo. "Then stop them."

Veron hesitated. *"Cese."*

Almost as one, the soldiers stopped the beating.

"Sálgalo de aquí."

"Xavier," she whispered his name, fighting back tears. His face was bloody, his clothes torn and his hands still tied.

The soldiers hauled him up. Almost unconscious, he still struggled, but they didn't seem to notice as they dragged him out the door, scrapping his knees in the dirt.

"It'll be okay," she promised, but he was already gone.

Xavier rolled over, groaning. How long had he been out? Surprised to find himself untied, he checked his watch by the dim light that filtered in from the lanterns outside the tent.

Midnight. He'd been unconscious for an hour and Bethany was nowhere in sight.

"Crap," he whispered. An hour might not seem like much, but for a trained man like Veron, an hour was plenty of time to inflict pain.

He thought of Bethany being interrogated. Tortured. Hurt. Or worse.

He had to escape. He had to get to Bethany. His muscles groaned as he staggered to his feet. Nothing felt broken, but he'd bet money he was going to have some spectacular bruises tomorrow.

Limping towards the opening of the tent, he pulled back the canvas and was greeted by two soldiers and the open end of a shotgun. He doubted it was loaded with something as innocuous as birdshot, but even birdshot at point blank range would leave a helluva hole.

"Vuelva adentro," the soldier snarled, ratcheting a shell into the chamber like a warning shot.

Xavier hesitated, his hands searching for a weapon that wasn't there.

"Ahora."

He couldn't save Bethany if he were dead. Frustrated, Xavier forced himself to do as the soldier demanded and stepped back inside. With a groan, he buried his hands in his hair. He hadn't felt this helpless since FARC took Eva.

He'd failed Eva that day. He'd been working in the bar and hadn't even realized they'd taken her until he got the phone call.

He'd be damned if he was going to fail Bethany. There were only two soldiers outside. He was sure Veron meant the lack of guards as an insult. That he considered Xavier less than a threat.

Arrogance, mistake number one. A pleased grin twisted Xavier's mouth.

It was time to take back control of their situation. He scanned the dark space for something he could make into a weapon, but there was no chair, no bed—nothing but a worn, forgotten blanket against the wall of the tent.

Unless he was able to transform it into an UZI, he was out of luck.

That left just himself and his skills. Walking over to the far side of the tent, he strained to listen. The camp was quiet.

"Xavier?"

Bethany. He whirled around, his beaten muscles screaming at the sudden, violent movement.

She stood in the doorway of the tent, the light behind her, leaving nothing but a silhouette. In four long strides, he crossed the tent and pulled her to him, relief as deep and solid as the bruises across his back. "Are you okay? Did Veron hurt you?"

Bethany shook her head, her cheek crushed against his chest. "He didn't a lay a finger on me." She looked up, her eyes lingering on his face. "I can't say the same for you, though."

"I've sustained worse in a bar fight."

Frowning, she stroked his cheek, her touch light and comforting as a cool pack against his flesh. His body sang with pleasure at having her safe. At being given another chance to protect her. He grasped her fingers, kissing the tips.

Her breath caught and her eyes widened. With a tentative touch, she slid her hand up his torso, stopping at his heart, her fingers spread outward.

"Your heart's pounding," she remarked, her voice raspy and just above a whisper.

He pressed his open palm over her sternum, mirroring her stance. Bethany's heart thumped like a bass against his hand. "So is yours."

God help him, he wanted to let himself go.

But there were consequences to his actions, and the desire he knew they felt wasn't real. It was a symptom of relief. Nothing more. They both deserved better.

He was going to have to be the strong one. Savoring the feel of her skin, he dragged his hand up her torso, smoothed her hair back, leaned in and kissed her forehead.

For a beat, there was nothing but awkward silence.

He crossed his arms over his chest. If he didn't, his treacherous arms might pull her back to him. "What happened?"

Bethany stared at him, confusion in her eyes.

He hoped she understood his sudden change, but he wasn't going to ask. He wasn't about to open up that conversation. "Bethany, what happened? What did he ask?"

Disappointment replaced confusion then she shrugged. "He asked about my job. Hollywood. Angelina Jolie."

"What did you say?"

"That I didn't know her."

Smart-ass. Xavier smiled despite the tension between them. "What else?"

Outside their tent, someone coughed, reminding Xavier that he and Bethany were anything but alone.

She opened her mouth to answer, and he shook his head, putting a finger over his lips then pointing to the blanket.

Bethany took a seat. "That's it. Details on what I was looking for in a location but otherwise, nothing *important*."

He didn't miss the stress in her words. They needed to talk without raising suspicion. He sat down then stretched out. "We should rest."

She hesitated.

He couldn't blame her. He'd rejected her moments ago.

She looked at him over her shoulder, her eyes lit with a wicked glint. "Of course." Lying down, she snuggled against him, her back fitted to his chest and her bottom against his groin and wiggled into him.

Xavier gritted his teeth as she moved, trying to get comfortable. "Do you mind?"

"No. Do you?"

It was going to be a long night. And they needed to talk, not tease each other. One hand on her hip, he rolled her away. "Turn over."

With a "humph," she faced him. Her hip pressed against his. There was no more wriggling.

Xavier pushed her long hair away, exposing her neck, and leaned in. She smelled like sweat and earth. "Did he believe you?" he whispered, his mouth pressed against her ear.

She shivered against him. "He wanted to, I know that."

"Good. We can use that against him."

She took a deep breath, her chest pushing against his. "What if Veron finds out who we are? What if wanting to believe isn't enough?"

He knew Bethany wanted him to say Veron wouldn't figure them out. But he hadn't lied to her yet. He'd teased, taunted and even charmed her but never lied, and he didn't plan to start now. "If he discovers who we are and why we are here, we'll go to jail."

"And Samantha?"

Did she need him to say what they both knew?

"What about Samantha, Xavier?"

"She'll remain FARC's prisoner." And so would Eva.

Bethany gasped at his bluntness and hearing the possibilities aloud even knocked the wind out of him. "You asked."

"I did. I even knew the answer." She twisted onto her back and stared at the top of the tent. He didn't have to be a genius to see he'd all but killed her hope of rescuing Samantha.

That wasn't what he wanted. He needed her optimism. Her passion. Without that, they might as well tell Veron who they were and be done with it. He took her chin in hand, turning her head toward him, her mouth inches from his. "I said he *might* find out who we are, but I didn't say he would. To do that would take days, and I don't plan on being here that long."

With exquisite slowness, she rolled toward him. Her mouth brushed his as if savoring the moment. Once. Twice. Three times.

Their kiss in the bar rushed back. How she pulled him to her, releasing the fierceness that lurked beneath her cool exterior. The strength that drove her to do whatever it took to find her sister.

Bethany's touch, her talk and even the way she walked reflected the confident woman beneath, the guide who was always sure of her footing.

He knew that woman. Traveled with her. Admired her.

This woman next to him, the one who hesitated with her mouth against his, was still the Bethany he had met just a few days ago. But also not her. It wasn't that she wasn't strong or wasn't fierce. She was all those things and more. But she offered something new. Something the Bethany from the bar didn't.

Vulnerability.

Her surprising openness pulled him to her. Made him toss aside good intentions and duty.

Her mouth brushed his again. He traced a path up her arm, over her shoulder and to the back of her neck. Untying the strip of leather from her now-messy braid, he unplaited it, letting her hair fall past her shoulders.

The strands were like silk against his fingers, and he buried them in the mahogany mass and pulled her tighter to him, urging her mouth open.

She breathed him in, and for a beat, he was lost in her. Lost in what she offered. He ran his tongue along her lower lip.

"Promise me," Bethany said against his mouth. "Promise me we'll get out of here."

He had no idea how he was going to get them out of the camp and no right to make such a claim. Duty reared it ugly head and struck a pact with hope.

As much as he wanted her, there would be no lovemaking. Not while she was vulnerable. But he'd give her everything else. His protection. His loyalty. And her family.

Using every ounce of strength, Xavier broke the kiss. "I promise."

* * *

"Major Veron wishes to speak with you."

Someone nudged Bethany, and she bolted upright, heart pounding. She breathed out the disorientation that came from being woken without warning and took in her surroundings.

A soldier stood at their feet, one hand at his side and a pistol in the other. The flap to the tent lay open and the morning light slanted across the ground.

"Speak to whom?" Xavier asked, sitting up behind her, his hand on her hip.

Last night's adventure rushed back. Their capture. Her conversation with Veron. The fear.

The way she had kissed Xavier. How he had held her. Falling asleep with his arms around her, keeping her close.

Oh, crap.

The memory both warmed and horrified her.

The soldier gazed past her. "The woman. Now."

"Like hell," Xavier growled in her ear. "You're not going. Not without me." He started to rise and the soldier cocked his weapon.

She could not go through the terror of seeing Xavier at gunpoint again. "Please," she whispered, wrapping her arms around his broad shoulders and holding him down with the weight of her body.

Xavier tried to shake her off, but she held firm. "I can't protect you if I'm not with you."

The feminine part of her melted at the words, but she shut that woman up. Now was not the time to go girlie. "If he wanted to hurt me, he'd have already done it."

The soldier put a hand on Bethany's shoulder.

"Please," she repeated. "I'll be fine."

Xavier hesitated, lips pressed tight as he looked up at the soldier. He rose. "No."

Why did he insist on being a macho pain-in-the-ass? She

was going to kill him herself. Still on the ground, Bethany watched the soldier. He shrugged.

She breathed a sigh of relief.

Bethany stood, stretching. The soldier gathered the burlap bags from the ground and put them over their heads. Fifteen stumbling, awkward minutes later, they stopped.

She strained to listen. Veron was talking to someone— probably their escort from the angry tones. The bag was removed from her head. Veron waited in front of her, looking as awake and pressed as if he'd had a full night's sleep. The escort remained, his gun trained on Xavier.

"What do you think?" Veron asked.

The back of her neck prickled. "What do I think of what?" she asked as her imagination roiled with the more negative answers—rape, torture, Xavier's head disconnected from his shoulders while she was forced to watch.

"The location, of course. It is beautiful, yes?"

For a heartbeat, Bethany stared at Veron, her brain processing the unexpected information. "The location?"

"My men searched the IMDb as you suggested. There was not much, but there was a mention of you working on a movie from last year. My men assure me it isn't something you could have forged yourself."

God bless IMDb.

Veron smiled, transforming him from a no-nonsense commander to starstruck fan, and she understood what had happened. She'd dealt with the same phenomena when she'd returned to Utah after her movie consultant position ended.

People thought she had an "in" with the Hollywood crowd. They launched into soliloquies at weird and inappropriate times, and one young guide had shoved a movie script she'd written into Bethany's backpack. All annoying considering she had as much "in" as a rock.

Not that she planned to crush Veron's perceptions of her

worth. In this situation there was only one choice—encourage it.

Veron continued, "Of course, I have calls out as well, but I am sure that you are who you say you are."

Her confidence slipped at the comment, but Bethany kept her smile cool. Standing behind her, Xavier touched her lower back. She gave a short nod of understanding. These people verified her consulting position, which was useful, but it was only a matter of time before they dug deeper and discovered the real reason she was here.

Then none of her Hollywood connections would matter. She and Xavier would spend the next ten years in a Colombian jail.

"So, what do you think?" Veron repeated, circling back to the original question. His eyes and tone betrayed his eagerness to be a part of the mythical Hollywood scene.

And she'd give it to him. By the shovel full.

Pursing her mouth and trying to appear as serious as possible, Bethany cocked her head and took in the scenery. From the thirty-foot waterfall to the stunning array of parrots that inhabited the trees, the clearing was an awe-inspiring example of what the world would be without man.

She walked over to the edge of the pool beneath the falls. "How deep is the water?" It was so clear that perception of depth was lost.

"Thirty feet beneath the falls."

She nodded. "Does it have a name?"

"Agua del murciélago."

"Water of…"

"Water of the bat," Xavier translated.

Water of the bat? Excitement rushed through her, making her tremble. The hostage that had brought her Samantha's location had mentioned it. She was sure of it.

"Named for the local bats," Veron explained. He pointed at

what looked like a cliff. "Over on the other side of the falls are caves. The bats have lived there for centuries."

Waterfall. Bats. Caves. She filed the information away, building a map in her head and matching it to the one she'd constructed. "How about up there?" Bethany gestured to the top of the falls, verifying what she hoped she knew. "What's up there?"

Veron stopped midstep. "You do not want to go that way, *señorita*."

"Why?" She fought to keep her feet from dancing beneath her.

"There is danger that way. Bad men who would kidnap you."

Did he mean FARC?

There wasn't anyone else around that she knew of. She glanced back at Xavier. His expression was one of bland concern. "Are they close?" she asked.

"Do not worry. They will not attack while my army is here." He squeezed her arm as if reassuring a small child.

"Thank you." More than you will ever know.

He smiled and, once again, appeared more like a hypnotized fan than leader of an army. He pulled her back into motion, gesturing for Xavier and the soldier to follow. "Come. There is much to see. I think you will find my jungle the perfect place to produce your show."

Bethany stayed close. "I think so, too."

Chapter 7

"Does wanting to duct tape his mouth shut make me a bad person?" Bethany asked Xavier, pulling aside the tent flap to watch Veron walk farther away.

They'd spent the majority of the day exploring the jungle, listening to Veron confess to his dream of being the next Tarantino.

Somewhere along the way, she'd shifted from being worried about being caught in a lie to being worried she might never escape the surprisingly yappy commander.

"No. I thought the same thing. Except it was a dirty towel tied too tight."

As boring and irritating as it was to have to listen to the commander, it proved one thing beyond a doubt. Veron believed her. At least until he heard differently.

By that time, they'd be gone. She hoped. Bethany waved at the two sentries guarding their tent then let the tent flap swing closed. "Well, I have good news."

"We're close to FARC? I know."

"Oh." That sucked the wind from her big announcement. "How?"

He shrugged and started scouting the edges of the tent, tugging the canvas, checking for weak spots in its assembly. "This is my jungle, as well. My people. There are no native tribes within fifty miles. Who else could it be?"

Her shoulders dropped. "Well, did you know it was the FARC camp that was holding Samantha?"

Xavier looked at her over his shoulder. "Are you sure?"

So he didn't know everything. It was a bit of a relief—not that she was keeping score. "I recognized the falls. They're on my map. We're less than two miles away."

Xavier rose and came toward her, his movements stiff but his dark eyes bright. Was he happy at the news or pissed? Bethany braced herself against his contradicting body language.

Wrapping his arms around her waist, he lifted her feet off the ground and twirled her in a circle.

Bethany pressed her head into his shoulder. Okay, happy it was.

He set her down at the third revolution and Bethany tottered on unsteady feet for a few seconds. "Glad I could accommodate."

"You did good." Xavier steadied her. "Though this would have all gone faster if you'd told me where we were going to begin with."

"You know why I couldn't do that," Bethany shot back.

"I'd have left you." His darks eyes bored into hers but there wasn't any animosity in them. Just good-natured teasing. "Just think it through, if I had, you wouldn't be here, wishing for duct tape."

"But you didn't and I am." She said with a grin, not begrudging the banter.

She felt she could afford it. He might know the location of the

FARC camp, there was no way he'd leave her behind. Not now. If he did, she'd end up in jail, and they both knew it.

"You are." He pushed a strand of hair from her face. Electricity rippled through her at the touch, and memories of last night surfaced. She'd all but forgotten them during the light of day and her preoccupation with Veron.

Now that they were alone with his hand in her hair and standing so close that she felt the heat of his skin, memories rushed back, refusing to be ignored.

Xavier's breathing deepened. His fingers wove their way through her hair, pulling her closer. "How do I keep you safe?"

A question she couldn't and wouldn't answer. At least not the way he wanted.

He kissed the top of her head and she steeled herself against the part of her that wanted to give in to weakness. It would be so easy to let him take care of her. "Me? I can take care of myself." She traced a path up his arm to his shoulder and lingered at the bruise that graced his cheek. "You're the one that managed to get beaten up."

He smiled. "Touché."

She smiled back, grateful he didn't argue the point. "I think the real concern is how am I going to protect you?" she teased. Rising on her toes, she licked her lower lip, taunting him.

Xavier leaned forward, brushing her lower lip with his mouth, taking the dare. "You're going to protect me?"

"Someone has to."

He hesitated then brushed her lips with his. "What is it that makes me want to kiss you?"

She sighed against his mouth. "My moxie."

"Moxie?"

"Tenacity. The kind of girl who does what she wants and be damned what other people think."

"Ah." He brushed her mouth with his again. "So, Señorita Moxie, what is it you want to do?"

She knew what he was thinking because it was the same thought circling through her mind, and it had nothing to do with escape or protection and everything to do with naked bodies.

"This," she said, wrapping her arms around his neck and pressing her mouth against his.

He pulled her lower lip with his teeth, making her groan, and his hands slid under her shirt and up her back.

Somewhere in her mind, she knew it was the worst timing in the world, but her body didn't care. She needed him. Wanted him.

No one else would do.

Outside of the tent, conversation rose. She might not understand the language but she knew an argument when she heard one. Xavier broke the kiss and put a finger again his mouth, signaling her to be quiet.

Great. Would they never catch a break?

Seconds later, one of the guards strode into the tent head down, cap over his eyes. Bethany stumbled backward, pushing herself away from Xavier, feeling like a wayward schoolgirl.

Xavier headed toward the soldier.

Crap, there was going to be another fight. At least it was one-on-one, or would be until the soldier called his friends. Bethany hurried over, hands outstretched to pull Xavier back.

Instead of cocking his hands back in a fist, Xavier pulled the soldier to him in a big hug, clapping the man on the shoulder and chuckling.

Bethany stopped midstep. "What—"

Xavier let him go and the man raised his head. "*Hola,* Bethany."

She hurried forward and wrapped her arms around him. "*Hola* yourself, Sebastian."

He squeezed her. "Did you miss me?"

"Of course," she said. "How did you find us?"

He shook his head. "I have to be quick," he whispered. "Tomas is north of the camp, waiting for you."

"How do you propose we get away?" Xavier asked.

"Tomas is going to create a distraction." Sebastian extracted a handgun from underneath his shirt and handed it to Xavier. "We have to go. Now."

As much as she wanted to escape, they couldn't go with just a few guns. "We'll need the rest of the gear. There's no way we can mount a rescue without it." Earpieces. Binoculars. They were all needed if she planned to rescue Samantha.

"What is she talking about?" Sebastian looked to Xavier.

Bethany realized he didn't know about the FARC encampment.

"The FARC camp where Samantha is being held is close," Xavier explained. "A few kilometers or more."

"We have to go after her," Bethany insisted.

Sebastian frowned. "It is too dangerous."

"Yes it is, without the gear," Bethany reiterated.

"There is no time. We have to go. Veron is on his way."

Crap. "Why?"

"Dinner, I think. He wants to impress you."

Now she really did want duct tape.

Sebastian turned to Xavier. "Talk some sense into her."

Bethany took a step back. She didn't need someone to talk sense into her. She needed weapons, gear and her sister. "You promised me," she reminded Xavier.

Xavier stared at her. "Do you know where the gear is being held?" he asked Sebastian.

"A tent on the other side of the camp."

"How many guards?"

"Two."

Xavier paced past her, a hand still in his hair. Bethany tensed. If Xavier decided to leave, she'd be on her own. There was no way she'd talk Sebastian into helping her. As much as he and Tomas were nice to her and even respected her, they were Xavier's men. They'd follow him to the ends of the earth.

They followed her because he told them to.

He stopped and Bethany held her breath.

"Do you remember Tecala?" he asked Sebastian.

Sebastian rolled his eyes, then smiled. "Of course."

"Same thing."

"What happened in Tecala?" Bethany inquired.

The men ignored her. "I'll tell Tomas," Sebastian stated, as he headed out the door. "See you in an hour."

"I am afraid I monopolized the conversation today in my eagerness," Veron apologized, handing Bethany a glass of wine.

That was an understatement.

"Tell me more about your experiences as a location scout."

She took the ceramic mug that served as a glass, trying to appear more relaxed than she felt. She hated not knowing a plan. But before Xavier could tell her what had happened in Tecala, an escort had arrived and taken her to Veron.

Now she sat with the Major, having dinner, waiting for all hell to break loose, and hoping her nerves held and that she didn't burst into hysterical giggles.

She took a large swallow of wine. It burned her throat. Whatever it was, it wasn't wine no matter what the bottle claimed. She held back a coughing fit. "Smooth."

Catching her breath, she set the mug down on the crate that served as their table. "There isn't that much to tell. I look for locations that are interesting and different. Safe but not too safe."

"What do you think of my jungle?" He took a seat in one of the camp chairs across from her.

Bethany hesitated. Now was the perfect time to get as much information as possible. She wondered if bringing FARC into the conversation would make him suspicious? Or would it be more suspicious not to mention them since they'd be of concern to a location scout. "There are issues with Colombia."

He leaned forward. "Such as?"

It was a test. She could feel it. Should she mention FARC? Or should she play dumb?

Fifty-fifty.

"FARC," she said, bracing herself.

Veron sighed and leaned back. "I wondered when they would come up in conversation."

She'd passed the test.

Outside, there was a shout. Was this the breakout? She tensed, poised to spring into action—whatever that might be.

Veron cocked his head, listened and then turned to her.

No, not yet.

She toasted Veron and sipped her drink. It tasted better. Much better. Making a getaway when she was in the dark on the details was hard enough. Getting drunk would make it more difficult. She set the glass down.

"So…FARC…of course, they come up," she said. "We do not want our contestants or executives kidnapped."

Veron nodded. "Understandable, but I can assure you of their safety."

"How can you assure that? People are kidnapped every day in Colombia."

He frowned. "I cannot argue the fact, but it shames me. I would show the world that Colombia is a good country with good people. *Endurance* would do this."

He meant it, Bethany realized. He did this for himself—the all-day-pay-attention-to-me marathon proved that—but for his country, as well.

She smiled. "It would help, I can't deny that." Leaning forward, she templed her hands in front of her. "But it will also bring attention to the kidnappings. Negative news sells, you know that."

He nodded.

Outside, there was more arguing, Veron listened, but this time, he held up his hand for silence. Unholstering his weapon, he rose.

"What is it?" Bethany stood, placing herself beside him, prepared to do whatever needed to be done.

"I do not know."

"FARC?"

His lips thinned. "Stay behind me. If it is FARC, I will protect you."

His concern would be sweet if she wasn't trying so hard to escape.

"Wait here." He headed toward the door, leaving her alone.

"Thank God." She followed, poking her head out the window. Soldiers ran around in packs, guns drawn.

She didn't hear any shots. What the hell were Tomas and Sebastian doing? Something low to the ground streaked by in the firelight.

"The jaguar?" She watched a group of soldiers rush past in its wake. "How the hell did they get it to enter the camp?"

"Meat," a voice said. "Lots of meat."

"Xavier?" He came from the back of the tent.

"Expecting someone else?" He handed her a handgun, his face grim and all business. "You have a full clip."

"Where did you get it?"

"Don't ask." He pointed toward another tent on the far side of the fire. "Stick to the shadows. We're going around. Sebastian will meet us there."

"Tomas?"

"Cover if we need it."

Good enough. And the plan was just crazy enough to work. Or get them killed.

Xavier moved along the shadows, his feet silent. Bethany trailed, staying in his footsteps. A soldier rushed past, missing them in his hurry to get in on the hunt.

She sighed in relief and hoped their run of luck would last. What felt like an eternity later, they arrived at their destination undetected. Xavier lifted up the canvas. "Go."

She slid inside. Outside, the central fire shadowed the sentries. Neither moved.

Xavier slid in beside her. "Let's get our gear and get the hell out."

She couldn't agree more. Crates stacked two feet deep and three high lined the sides. Veron was prepared for war.

She spotted no packs. "A light would be good."

Outside, men shouted. The sentries moved and one came toward the tent. Their luck had run out. Bethany raised her weapon.

Stay out. Stay out. Stay out. She chanted the phrase in her head, but the sentry opened the door and stepped inside.

Xavier put his hand on her weapon. "Took you long enough."

"I was watching the show."

Sebastian. Again. "Crap, you're good at blending," she whispered.

"One of my many skills," he remarked, the usual joking tone replaced by a seriousness that surprised her. "The packs are over there. Behind the crates."

She and Xavier hurried to the crates while Sebastian guarded the door.

She slung hers on one shoulder, trusting that their gear was intact.

"Let's go. Hurry," Xavier said, holding the edge of the tent back up. Bethany shoved her pack out. Then the others.

"Damn," Sebastian said.

She looked up, and once again, the central fire highlighted the men outside.

The other sentry was coming into the tent.

"Go!" Xavier shoved her through the small opening. "Run!"

"Where's Sebastian?" Bethany asked, bending over to catch her breath when Xavier stopped. They hadn't gone far, but adrenaline made her heart pump as if she'd run a marathon.

"Here" a voice echoed in the dark.

She'd grabbed her pack before they escaped into the jungle and had been so intent on not falling in the dark that she hadn't noticed the other member of their team was ahead of them.

"Is everyone here?" Xavier asked.

"Yes." She recognized Tomas's voice and followed it. The fourth and final member stepped out from behind a tree.

"Any pursuit?" Xavier inquired.

"Not yet."

"You sure?" Bethany prodded.

"Positive," Tomas replied. Sebastian handed him a pack.

"You two know the drill," Xavier stated. "Rendezvous is at the FARC encampment. North side."

"See you in twenty-four," Sebastian confirmed. Then he and Tomas went back the way they'd come.

"What are they doing?" Bethany asked. "They're supposed to be running from the army. Not toward them."

"Leading Veron and his men away from us," Xavier replied. "They're more skilled at this."

"You mean more skilled than me."

Lights and shouting filtered through the jungle. Veron and his men weren't far. A shout echoed—

Bethany flinched. Had they spotted Sebastian and Tomas—

Gunfire followed.

"It doesn't matter what the reason is," Xavier said.

At least he didn't lie, though part of her wished he'd allow himself the occasional fib. Taking her hand, he guided her through the bushes and grass. The taller trees of the canopy loomed large a few feet in front of them. Xavier's words repeated through her head. *Only fools traveled in the jungle at night.*

Fools or the desperate.

He hesitated at the edge. "They won't follow us in here. Don't touch anything. Stay close." Two steps later, they were beneath the trees and on what looked like a game trail. Dangerous but clearer and quieter than tromping through the dead leaves that covered the canopy floor.

Five feet inside and the change was immediate. The heat soaked her as thoroughly as a wall of water. The weight of the air pushed down on her, and the scent of moss and decay almost overwhelmed her.

"Is escaping into the jungle part of the Tecala plan?" Bethany questioned. Glancing upward there was nothing but darkness. Damn, the jungle was creepy at night.

"Sort of."

"What do you mean, sort of?" She tripped, catching herself against a tree. Her hand slipped on the slick bark and something stabbed it. Yelping, she yanked her hand away and tripped again.

"Are you hurt?" Xavier grabbed her before she fell.

"I'm okay", she replied even as her hand throbbed to painful life. She grimaced, thinking about Tomas's burrowing bug story. It's a story, she told herself. She did not have a bug working its way into her skin.

Her hand could wait. A strap from her pack brushed it, and she clenched her teeth to keep from hissing in pain then pulled her hand close so nothing else could touch it.

Voices carried through the heavy air. Closer, she was sure of it. But there was no light to give away their pursuers' position.

Hell, her hand would have to wait. "I thought they weren't supposed to follow us in here," Bethany whispered.

"They're not," Xavier growled. "They're better than I thought."

"You don't have to be nice," she said. They both knew why the soldiers changed tactics—her shout when she slipped and hit the tree.

"Stay quiet." He led her off the game trail and under the canopy. Fifty feet in, he pulled her behind a tree. "Stay here. Stay quiet. And for God's sake, stay hidden. If I'm not back in thirty minutes, go home."

Home? She opened her mouth to argue but he was already gone.

With a huff of frustration, Bethany remained kneeling and tried to ignore the bugs that crawled around her and over her. She brushed something off her arm, shuddering.

Damn, she hated bugs.

Time crawled as she waited and the voices grew closer. One in particular sounded excited, and she perked up at the tone.

Had they found something? Xavier? A trail?

Keeping low, she peeked around the trunk. There were lights on the game trail but no shouting. One of the lights swung her way, and she ducked behind the tree and shut her eyes.

There's nothing here. Nothing here. No one.

She was a moron for looking. And if she escaped detection, she promised herself she'd listen next time. She wouldn't peek or give in to her curiosity. She'd sit and be quiet.

Please God, let there be a next time.

There was a crackling behind her, but before she could react, a dark shadow put its hand over her mouth. She bit down hard.

He didn't let go. "Time to go. And less biting would be nice."

Xavier. She relaxed her jaw. Using his wrist as a prop, she wavered to her feet, trying to ignore her throbbing palm. "Sorry."

Taking her hand, he guided her back to the path. The soldiers were gone, working back the way they'd came.

"Stay close," he whispered, heading into the jungle, increasing their pace until they were running in the dark.

Chapter 8

"How are you holding up?"

Her hand hurt, her nerves were shot and the thought of leaving Sebastian and Tomas to draw Veron away because she sucked at jungle guiding both pissed her off and made her sick to her stomach. "I'm fine."

Xavier slowed to a walk, and Bethany took the opportunity to glance over her shoulder. There was no sign of their pursuers. No sound besides the screeches and howls that had become familiar over the past two days.

Xavier stopped. "We'll camp here for the night."

"Is it safe?"

"Safe enough. Besides, I don't want to cross a river at night unless we have to."

Bethany cocked her head and pulled the sound of moving water from the jungle noises that assaulted her ears. One more push through the leaves and she found herself standing at its banks.

Despite the break in the canopy overhead, the darkness was complete, and Bethany sensed that there was no sloping, sandy bank at her feet.

Something crawled over her arm and she brushed it off. Another took its place. "There are bugs everywhere." Now that they'd stopped moving, she and Xavier were fast becoming something new and exciting to climb.

Her hand throbbed harder.

"Let's pitch the tent," Xavier declared. "Fast. And away from the game trail. I don't want to run into the jaguar again or any of his healthier friends."

She shuddered, grateful they had carried one of the tents because she doubted that they'd build a fire, and she didn't want to spend the night fending off six- and eight-legged animals instead of sleeping.

Moving off the trail, they pitched the tent in minutes. Bethany tossed both packs to the back and crawled inside, flicking off bugs as she went.

Xavier zipped the tent closed and fell beside her. "Damn, it's crawling out there."

She smiled in the dark. "Does it *bug* you?"

He groaned at the pun.

"Couldn't resist," she teased, chuckling. Something tickled her cheek. and she brushed it away, hissing at the sharp pain when her palm brushed against her hair.

"What's wrong?" Xavier asked.

For a moment, she considered saying nothing but being in constant and increasing pain would slow them down. She'd done plenty of that already. "It's my hand," she admitted. "When I fell, something either bit me or stuck me."

Xavier didn't swear or castigate her. She heard him rummaging through his pack and seconds later, he flicked on a flashlight.

The nylon walls of the tent glowed. "Is that smart?" she pointed out, nodding at the light.

"No." He held out his hand and she put out hers palm up. The fleshy part below her thumb was red. "But leaving a wound untended in the jungle is even dumber. You know that."

He pulled it closer, frowning.

"Are there…" Bethany hesitated. "Eggs?"

"No eggs." He glanced up, his face highlighted by the flashlight like a Halloween lantern. "Tomas got to you, didn't he?"

She nodded. "What is it? What did I touch?"

He laid her hand in her lap and went back into his pack. "No idea, but it doesn't look like a bug bite." He pulled out a pair of tweezers. "It looks like a very nasty thorn."

She held her hand out again, looking away. She had dealt with other people's wounds without a problem. She'd bound broken bones, applied pressure to stop arterial blood flow and once, she had stitched a large gash closed with dental floss.

But her own body was where she wussed out.

"Hold this." Xavier handed her the scissors. The tweezers touched her flesh. She flinched.

"Hold still. I haven't done anything yet."

"Yet? That's comforting."

Eyes squeezed half-shut, she peeked through her lashes at the proceedings with both horror and fascination.

"Just a minute," Xavier proclaimed, using the pointed metal ends to probe into her flesh. She hissed in pain, jerking her hand away.

He glared at her. "Damn it, Bethany. I have got to get that out."

"I'm trying."

"Try harder unless you want to do it."

She shook her head. The one thing worse than someone else trying to fix her was trying to fix herself. A part of her hoped that in a pinch, she'd be able to do what was needed.

Yet here she was, letting Xavier fix the situation for her.

But this wasn't a pinch.

With a sigh of sympathy, he brushed her cheek. "Trust me."

"I do." And she did. Most of the time.

"Take a deep breath," he said. "In."

She inhaled.

"Exhale."

She breathed out.

"Now give me your hand and keep breathing. Focus on your breathing."

She held out her hand and did as instructed. Xavier held her hand, nothing more. "Keep breathing."

She breathed deep, trying to keep her attention on the sounds of the air pushing in and out of her body.

"I'm going to take the thorn out," he described. "It won't hurt."

"Okay," she whispered. She believed him. He was a rebel, a leader and a mercenary. But he was also gentle, strong and would take care of her if she let him. She didn't doubt that for a second.

"Breathe."

She felt the same pricking as she before and took a deep breath. Just breathe. She inhaled.

"Done." He let go her hand.

Bethany exhaled with a whoosh. "Done?"

He grinned at her, and she pointed the flashlight to his palm. In the center was a small thorn with barbed edges. "What is it?"

"No idea," he replied. "But I think you'll be able to keep the hand."

"Funny." Bethany smacked him on the shoulder with her good hand, but her wounded hand was feeling better already. "Should we put something on it?"

Reaching past her, he unzipped the tent a few inches and tossed the thorn outside. "A little antibiotic," Xavier said, rummaging in the pack again and coming back with a small tube and a bandage. "Hand out."

She wiggled her fingers at him.

Xavier grabbed her wrist with a chuckle. "You did good," he noted, smearing the ointment onto the wound. She noticed that the redness was already fading.

"Maybe," she responded, warming at the praise even though she knew she'd acted anything but good.

"Everybody has their issues," he declared, smoothing the bandage over the wound. "You didn't let it stop you. That is what's important."

"Well, it wasn't like I had a choice," she observed, her world spiraling in to center on his touch.

His thumb stroked her palm in a careless gesture that made her shivers coil outward. She swallowed hard, but the building desire refused to fade.

"We should go to sleep," she said.

Did he have a clue what he did to her?

"We should," he agreed, his voice catching.

Bethany glanced from where their hands met to Xavier's dark eyes. He needed her, as well. Without pain and fear as a distraction, memories of last night rolled over her. Her body curled up with Xavier's as they shared the burden of fear.

And the taste of his mouth and the strength in his touch.

Oh, this was bad.

He took the light from her hand. "Sleep is a good idea."

She knew that he meant anything but that.

He flicked off the light.

The darkness was complete.

Sitting in the blackness, Xavier kissed Bethany's fingertips. It had been over a year since he'd been with a woman. Before then, there had been sex with women he had cared for, but those moments of two bodies coming together was mutual satisfaction and nothing more.

Bethany was different. Until he had met her, he hadn't

known what he wanted in woman. He thought he knew. Sweet. Kind. Smart. Sexy. His former lovers were all those things. So was Bethany.

But he wanted more. He wanted strength. Courage. Someone who valued honor and family as much as he did. A companion in all ways.

And he'd found that in Bethany. Being with her would never be just sex. Could never be just sex.

"Xavier?" Bethany whispered his name in the dark. She wove her fingers through his.

Leaning over, he traced a path up her arm and tangled his fingers in her hair. "I'm going to make love to you," he murmured, giving her the choice to turn him down and praying to God that she wouldn't.

"I know."

He heard her breath quicken.

"You can say no if you choose."

She covered the hand on her cheek with her bandaged one. "Make love to me."

He slid his hand to the back of her neck and pulled her to him, meeting her halfway. Slowly, he traced her lower lip with his tongue. She tasted like salt and desire and opened to him without hesitation.

Damn, he wanted to kiss her forever. Kiss every inch of skin from the top of her head to the tips of her toes and then work his way up again.

Untangling his hand from hers, he slid it up the back of her shirt. Soft skin covered muscle that came from hiking and working in the wilderness.

He wished he could turn on the light. See her beautiful back, her sleek body and watch her flush when he was inside her. The thought of entering her made him groan.

She giggled.

He smiled. He'd never heard her giggle before. It was an unexpectedly girlish sound, and one he wanted to hear more often.

She ran her hand up his thigh until she touched his erection. "Mine," she whispered, squeezing him through the fabric of his pants.

He groaned again.

Bethany smiled at the sound, enjoying the feel of Xavier twitching beneath her hand. It was heady, having that much power over him.

"Yours?" Xavier asked.

"Yes." She squeezed him again.

"Vixen." With a firm hand, he pushed her back onto the sleeping bag. There was a zipping sound as he opened the side panels of the tent, leaving the mosquito mesh in place. The sounds of the night filled the small space.

Then another zipping sound caught her attention. She leaned up on her elbows. "What are you doing?"

"Protection."

"You brought protection?" She didn't think he'd brought it for her since Sebastian had brought their gear, but it made her wonder.

"For water," Xavier explained.

"Water?"

"A condom can hold a gallon of water. In a pinch, we can use one for transport."

"A condom as a water bottle. Wow, that's hot," she teased.

"If all it takes is a condom full of water to arouse you, wait until you see what I do with a sock," Xavier said, chuckling.

Bethany giggled again. It felt so good to know she could laugh with him. This wasn't just sex, and it should be a cause for celebration.

The air shifted as he moved to her side. "You are so beautiful," he whispered, leaning over to kiss her neck.

She arched upward, letting her hands roam over his shoulders. "How can you tell? It's pitch black. I might have a weird deformity."

Xavier chuckled. "I am sure your body is perfect, but that wasn't what I was talking about." He slid both hands under her shirt, drawing tiny circles on her skin, and moving toward her shoulders. Taking a moment to rub the stiffness from her muscles, he pulled her shirt over her head. Leaning over her, he kissed the skin over her heart. "I was talking about this." He kissed her again. "*This* is beautiful."

For a moment, she thought it might break at his kindness and her own duplicity. Her laughter faded.

Then he kissed his way up her chest, over her shoulder to her neck, skimmed her lips and kissed her forehead. "And this," he said. "*Muy bonita.*"

She didn't deserve this or him, but she didn't care. She wanted him. Wanted to be who he thought she was. She pulled him to her mouth and felt his smile as he kissed her. His hands roamed over her torso, skimmed her sides and slid her bra off her shoulders.

"Impressive," she said, tossing the scrap of material to the corner above her head. "I didn't even feel you unhook it."

He chuckled then did the same to the rest of her clothes until she was naked in the dark. Bethany wriggled, both exhilarated and nervous to be so exposed in both mind and body.

The swish of clothes told her that he was undressing, and the sound of a wrapper ripping told her what was about to happen next. Her breath quickened and body tightened at the thought of Xavier inside her, her hands on his shoulders and her legs wrapped around his hips.

Moments later, he lay next to her—heated skin against heated skin, hip to hip. He stroked her back again and kissed her neck. "I can't wait," he whispered.

"I wasn't asking you to."

Rolling her over, he parted her thighs with his knee. "This is just to take the edge off," he whispered, sliding into her.

"Oh, God," Bethany groaned as her body tightened around him. It had been too long since she'd been with a man. She was going to topple over before she had time to enjoy the sensations that pulsed through her.

He moved inside her with a slowness that pushed her closer to the edge, and she wrapped her arms around his shoulders, not wanting the moment to end.

"Tu boca es una dulce tentación," he whispered, kissing her in the dark. He thrust again, and she bit her bottom lip as her body tightened into a familiar spiral.

Not yet. Not yet.

"Let go, Bethany," Xavier muttered. Reaching between them as he stroked her with his thumb. "Let go."

Her body didn't give her a choice as a climax rushed over. Bethany arched upward, fingers digging into Xavier's back while she clenched her jaw to keep from crying out.

She raked her nails down him, and in the recesses of her mind, knew that taking the edge off her desire for him was a hopeless fantasy. She wanted to teeter on the edge forever. Instead, he remained deep inside her as he pulled her upward, raking her along his hips and prolonging her climax, and from the groan that echoed through the tent—his own agony.

Finally, she relaxed beneath him and he kissed her forehead. "That was amazing." She lifted her chin and kissed him back.

The scent of sex and sweat hung between them. He thrust into her again, making her gasp. "You assume it's over."

"It's not?"

He withdrew, and this time, there was nothing slow or gentle about the way he entered her. "It's not."

Bethany wrapped herself around him. He made love to her until another climax claimed her, and then he let go, joining her.

Bethany lay on her side, watching Xavier sleep in the morning light that filtered through the canopy and into their small tent.

Being careful not to wake him, she inched her hand toward him and pushed a strand of hair from his forehead and traced a thin scar that started on his temple and went into his hairline. Last night had been amazing. She'd never had anyone make love to her with such intensity or thoroughness. She wanted more. She wanted Xavier. He made her feel like the person she pretended to be.

And that simple fact was what made the future too painful to contemplate. When he found out what she'd done. The lies she had told. The money she didn't have.

He'd see the real Bethany, and he'd hate her. She'd never have him again. Never have that feeling again.

The thought made her heart hurt. She curled into a ball.

She had no choice. Not if she wanted to free Samantha. She pressed a hand against her sternum, pushing the pain down.

"You okay?" Xavier asked. He squeezed her shoulder.

She looked up. "You're awake."

He kissed her forehead in a way that was now familiar and decidedly Xavier. "I am."

"We should go," she said. "Veron will be looking for us as soon as the sun is up." If they didn't leave, she'd find herself on her back again. While her body wanted him, she wasn't sure her heart could take it.

Xavier curled a strand of her hair around his finger and pulled her to him. "In a minute."

Her gaze traced his hand, worked its way up his arm to his eyes.

"Do you know what I want?" he queried.

She did, and there was no time. Still, she found herself inhaling his scent and unable to pull away. "What do you want?"

Rolling onto his back, he pulled her with him until she was astride his hips, his erection between her legs. "This."

He skimmed her sides with his palms then drew patterns with his fingertips. Her insides melted and she wanted him, guilty conscience be damned.

She'd deal with that later.

Leaning forward, she flattened her hand over his heart. They stared into each other's eyes until she blinked, unable to stand the intensity of his gaze.

She was a fool.

"Bethany." He pulled her forward, taking her nipple in his mouth and biting it just enough to make her breath catch.

He bit harder, one hand weaving through her hair to keep her from pulling away, making her jump.

"Xavier." Tossing her hair from her face, she grabbed for his pack. "Where the hell are those water holders?"

Beneath her, he laughed. "Front pocket. In a hurry?"

"Me?" One-handed, she unzipped the pocket and felt inside.

"You." He smiled up at her.

She touched a familiar plastic square. Pulling out a condom, she sat up.

Xavier grinned up at her. "You're on top. I guess that makes you in charge."

"I guess it does." Bethany bit her lip and placed a hand on each side of Xavier's thighs, leaning back. "Touch me."

He traced a path from her knee to her thigh then stroked her wetness, sending a ripple through her muscles.

"Oh, God," Bethany groaned. This was a bad idea. She wasn't in control, and they both knew it.

He stroked her again and again and the ripples grew and expanded until her muscles shook.

Then Xavier shifted beneath her, and before she could protest, she found herself on her back again. "You never said what I had to use to touch you," Xavier whispered in her ear and kissed his way down her torso.

"Oh, hell," she muttered watching as he parted her thighs.

He glanced up at her, grinning. His eyes fixed on hers, he stroked her with his tongue.

The climax that tore through her was immediate and hard.

She bit her hand to keep from crying out and tried to twist away. It was too much. But Xavier held her hips, forcing her to remain still while her orgasm washed over her in what felt like never-ending waves.

Just when the ecstasy became painful to bear, he let her go and slid up her body. The familiar sound of a condom opening made her hold her breath in anticipation, and seconds later, he was inside her, his hands touching her everywhere. She closed her eyes and reveled in the weight of him and the shifting of muscles beneath his skin. The way he held her tight, keeping them as close as possible. The whispered words of Spanish that needed no translation.

He slowed, his muscles contracting as Bethany's hips tilted higher. His hands fisted in her hair, and he groaned against her neck as his body spasmed. Finally, he relaxed, keeping his weight on his forearms while he looked down at her, smiling.

Bethany skimmed his back with her nails, tickling the skin. Some days, she loved being a woman. "Good morning."

Chuckling, Xavier raised his head and kissed her. "Good morning." Still inside her, he stared down at her. His eyes were dark and deep and reached all the way into her heart.

Oh, yeah, he was going to hate her soon. There was no doubt about that. She wrapped her legs around him, keeping him close and wanting the morning to last forever.

Chapter 9

"Hold." Xavier held up his hand.

Bethany stopped midstep. The day was more than half over, but she felt as if they'd made little progress through the thick jungle. Crossing the large stream had been difficult with its moss-covered rocks and fast-moving waters, and while there wasn't brush under the canopy to slow them, there were fallen branches, dead trees and more moss.

Moss covered everything. A part of her was convinced that if they stopped, it would take root on her.

"What's going on?"

He held his hand up again. "Shh."

Was it the damn, tenacious jaguar? FARC?

Xavier unhooked his pack, and let it slide down his arms to the ground with a small thud. He cupped his ear, amplifying whatever it was that caught his attention.

Bethany unhooked her pack, setting it next to his. Whatever he heard, it didn't seem to bode well.

"Stay here," he whispered. Dropping to the ground, he wormed his way through the foliage.

Stay? After being with her for the past few days, did he really think she was the kind of woman who would wait while he went off and acted the alpha male?

The pitfalls of sex, she realized. Now that he'd made love to her, he wanted to protect her even more. Since they'd left the tent, he'd taken point. Moved slower than they did before. He'd even offered her a hand over the fallen trees.

Crap. He'd turned her into a girl and not in a good way.

But she'd never been the helpless damsel, and she wasn't about to start acting like one. He wanted to be the alpha male? She wasn't going to let him forget that for every alpha male, there was the alpha female counterpart.

And that was her. Besides, the thought of him going alone made her shiver. What if something happened to him?

Bethany sunk to the ground. Keeping back and being careful of her hand, she followed Xavier as he wormed his way over dead leaves and moss-covered rocks.

He stopped, glanced over his shoulder, frowned and shooed her back.

She shook her head.

Go back, he mouthed. *Wait.*

No. She held her ground. At least he couldn't yell at her. Not unless he planned to announce their presence to whatever it was that caught his attention.

He shook his head in what she was sure was irritation then continued to crawl forward.

Being careful not to move the foliage around her, she paralleled Xavier. A scarlet and blue beetle scuttled over her hand, and she watched it run away.

He stopped and she crawled beside him. "Oh, my God," she whispered. A foot in front of them, the jungle came to an abrupt end and the earth opened up in a crack that ran out of sight.

As wide as a football field was long, the chasm cut through the mountain. The red rock that colored the sides gave it the appearance of a large wound. Trees and foliage hung from the sides. She spotted the flash of scarlet wings of a macaw in one of the trees on the other side.

Herida roja? Her heart thumped hard inside her chest with fear and excitement. If she was correct and this was *herida roja,* then FARC was somewhere on the other side. The question was, how close? Were they a single kilometer away, five or ten? Either way, it was close enough.

I'm coming, Samantha.

She followed the edge of the gorge with her eyes, stopping when she reached a wooden bridge spanning the gorge. Whoever built the structure had done so with the least amount of effort and skill to make it walkable.

She didn't care. It could be made of toothpicks held together with yarn and she'd cross it to get to Samantha. She rose to her knees for a better view and found herself jerked back hard enough to taste dirt.

She yanked her arm from Xavier's grasp. "What is your problem?"

As if in answer to her question, two men stepped into view on the other side of the gorge. Dressed in brown pants, tan shirts and carrying what looked like UZIs, they walked the edge of the crevasse, talking and watching.

FARC sentries.

Now she noticed the faint sounds of clinking and a murmur that might be more people talking. She looked upward. A smudge of smoke curled a path into the sky.

They weren't just close to the FARC camp. They were across from it. She couldn't have planned it better with a compass.

Her heart pounded harder, so loud in her ears she was sure the men across the river heard it, as well. They'd found the camp where her sister was being held. For a moment, she forgot to breathe.

Xavier tapped her shoulder, motioning her to leave. In tandem, they pushed themselves backward until they were again with their packs and could stand with little chance of being discovered.

"What the hell was that about?" Xavier demanded. "Are you trying to get us caught?"

Bethany's cheeks burned with embarrassment. She should have been more observant. Xavier counted on her to be as smart and savvy as she claimed to be. Instead, she'd allowed herself to become lost in her thoughts of Samantha. "It won't happen again."

"Damn straight, it won't."

Bethany crossed her arms over her chest. She knew that tone and that look, and she was not having this conversation for what felt like the hundredth time. "You just can't let it go, can you?"

He opened his mouth to answer, and she held up her hand. "Don't bother," she said, trying to head off the argument before it even began.

"I want you to wait. We both know it's for the best."

"You're not leaving me here. I am not waiting while you rescue Samantha. None of that is going to happen. So don't even try to push it."

"Okay," he agreed.

That was too easy.

He continued, "At least you wait here while I find a way across. I don't want any more screwups. Not this close to their camp."

While he looked for a way across? The bridge was out of the question, what with FARC guarding the rim of the gorge.

Which meant he'd have to hike until he found a place to cross. She knew that if she let him leave, the next time she would see him, he'd be on the other side.

Did he really think she was that gullible?

She bit her tongue, forcing herself to remain calm. "I'm going with you."

"No. You're not."

She cared for Xavier, and her feelings grew deeper the more she learned. She wasn't going to deny that, not even to herself. But Samantha was her sister, and it would take more than a budding romance and one night and morning of lovemaking to keep her from participating in the rescue. Besides, she'd come too far and sacrificed too much to wait on the sidelines.

She'd waited long enough.

"Unless you tie me up, yes I am."

For a moment, Xavier looked tempted. He took a step toward her.

Bethany flattened a palm against his chest and looked up at him, daring him to try. "Leave me and I'll try to cross the bridge," she dared. "I swear it. My sister is on the other side of that gorge and I'm not going to wait here like a good little girl while she needs me."

"You'll slow us down."

"Us?" She flicked her gaze from side to side to make her point. "I don't see anyone here but you and me."

"Sebastian and Tomas will be here. Today or tomorrow."

"Whatever." She didn't care if the entire Colombian army marched behind him, she was going, and no one, not even Xavier, was taking this from her. "She won't go with you," Bethany claimed. "Not without me."

"She will."

"Are you willing to take that chance? Can you take that chance? She might raise a fuss and then you'd be caught."

"I would not be caught."

"What if you are?" Bethany asked. "You wouldn't be held hostage. I think you'd be made into an example."

Xavier didn't respond, and she realized his own sense of

safety was the wrong way to go if she wanted to convince him to take her—again. He wasn't a man who worried about himself. He worried about others. He was a good man. The best man she knew. But what made him strong also made him vulnerable and gave her ammunition.

"You might not care if you live or die, but I go with you or no cash. No Eva. That was the deal."

Bitch.

He didn't call her a bitch, but the way he looked at her—jaw clenched and eyes hard as stone—said it for him.

"This is as good a place as any to cross." Xavier dropped his pack from his back. They'd hiked along the gorge for three hours, but there wasn't another bridge to be found and they were losing time that they didn't have.

He hadn't said anything to Bethany, but with the Colombian army so close, FARC would be moving the hostages soon. In fact, he was surprised they hadn't done so already.

Give the terrorists another day and it would be all over. Samantha would be gone and he'd lose Eva, as well.

"How do we manage that? Fly?" Bethany asked. She walked toward the edge of the gorge, stopping a few feet away. A few hundred feet down, the white water echoed up the sides and a strong wind tossed her dark hair around her shoulders. Gathering the mass, she plaited it into a quick braid.

It was a simple, unconscious movement but it was those graceful, innate gestures that drew him to Bethany. Opened up pieces of him that he'd never bothered with before. Not that he hadn't wanted to, but there was never time. The little things she did made him want to make the time. The way she rolled her eyes when she thought he was wrong. The way her nose wrinkled when she glared at him, which was often.

Now this. Long hair, flying like water, and her strong hands, taming the strands.

Dammit, he wanted to stay angry with her. So far, that seemed to be impossible, when she was trying so damn hard.

During the hike, she'd teased him. Cajoled. Talked. Tried everything to jolly him. A part of him admired her tenacity and cheered it with an enthusiasm he couldn't show.

God help him, he was falling in love with the pain-in-the-ass and there was no way he could stay angry. Not knowing that.

She turned to him, hair in a messy braid, sun on her skin, and as much as she didn't like the jungle, looking like she was in her element. Unzipping his pack, he pulled out his longest length of rope and its thrower.

"What's that?" she asked, walking over.

"Line thrower."

"That's the name?"

He cocked his head and looked at her. He might not be angry any longer but it didn't have to mean he'd let her off the hook that easily. "That's what it does. Throws a line."

She shrugged. "It's kind of dull."

"What do you suggest?"

"The Zippy 3000?"

"Nope. Just *line thrower.*" He untied his rifle and clipped the thrower to the top. "Besides, if we changed it we'd have to rename everything," he teased with a smile.

She hesitated then smiled back. "We could call the rifle the Bullet Bringer," Bethany suggested.

He liked the idea but there was no way he was going to admit it. "Let's not." Xavier tied the end of the rope to the ring on the end of the spearhead.

"What are *we* doing?" Bethany prompted.

He didn't miss her emphasize on the "we" and let it go. "This goes into a tree on the other side, taking the line with it. When it's embedded, I yank the rope, the edges of the spear head slide out, locking it in."

She licked her lips, eyes dilated so wide that the green was all but lost. "And then we go across?"

He nodded. Was she scared? Excited? "Yes."

"Climbing?"

Climbing hand over hand was a helluva lot harder than it looked. It was even worse on a rope at three hundred feet. "There are rollers in the bag," he said. "We zip-line across."

"That's a long way across and a long way down," she noted, looking past him.

When she turned back, her skin was as pale as paper, giving him his answer.

"Are you sure you can do this?" Xavier asked. If she panicked during the crossing, they were both screwed and taking her across in tandem with him wasn't an option. The line wouldn't hold their combined weight. "Once you start, you can't stop."

"I'm going," she snapped back, her jaw tight.

"I didn't ask you not to," Xavier commented, his voice flat.

She raised her stubborn chin at him. "I'll be fine."

Stubborn pain-in-the-ass. He returned to prepping the gear. He didn't argue because there wasn't a point. Hell, she was worse than Eva, and he hadn't thought that was possible.

Eva. He clenched his hands into fists. He hated being helpless when it came to his sister. Wished he didn't have to take Bethany's money.

Others took money for rescue and mocked him for taking just enough to cover expenses. Now, he'd taken more and even though it was for Eva, it didn't feel good.

Inside, he felt as if he'd become the mercenary that people thought he was.

"Let's do this." Xavier handed Bethany the free end of the rope. "Tie this off."

She tied the rope to a sturdy tree and then tugged with her full weight to make sure it would hold.

He nodded in approval then faced the gorge. This was going to be tough. The width of the gorge was at the edge of the range of the line thrower. If he didn't get a solid hit on a tree, they'd have to go back and use the bridge, which wasn't an option at all.

Dropping to one knee, he sighted his target through the scope and squeezed the trigger.

The line zipped out, hissing as the metal barb arced across the gorge and impaled itself into the tree. Praying for luck, he checked it through the sight. The head embedded itself far enough that the side barbs disappeared into the wood.

Nice. He put the rifle down and yanked the line to set the barbs. "You sure you want to do this?" he asked again, giving her one last chance to back out.

Not that she would.

"Positive."

Of course she was. He removed the rollers and harness from his pack and tossed her a set. "Gear up."

She slipped into her harness, and he checked it out, pulling at the seams. The webbing looked good. No sign of wear. But the gear wasn't used that much. Instances like this were few and far between.

"I'll go first," he said. "The rollers are easy to work. Watch." Shouldering his pack on, he stepped up to the edge of the gorge, attached the rollers then clipped onto them. He looked over his shoulder. "See this?" He tapped the crank on the lower side of the roller. "If it stops, turn this. It's a bitch, but you can do it. It'll move the rollers by hand."

"Do you think it'll stop?" Bethany asked.

He shook his head. "No, we have gravity on our side. It's why I picked this spot. It gives us a downward angle."

She licked her lips. "Good."

He almost felt sorry for her, but none of this would be needed if she were more sensible.

"Xavier?" Bethany stepped in front of him.

She smiled a crooked, shaky grin and he couldn't help but feel sorry for her. "Yes?"

She leaned forward and kissed him. Her mouth was soft against his. "Be careful."

He cupped her face in his hands. "It'll be okay. You'll be okay. I promise. This is easy. Just like an amusement park ride."

She nodded and stepped away.

His blood racing, Xavier stepped to the edge. His skin tingled in anticipation. He didn't often get the chance to zipline, but it never got old. Never lost its thrill. "It's just like flying," he described. "Don't look down. Don't panic. Just enjoy the ride." With a push, he launched himself over the gorge, the familiar spike of fear washed over him at the initial leap. Would the barb hold? Would the rope break? Would he fall to his death?

The spike of fear lasted less than a second as sheer joy replaced it. Moments like this made the job. He didn't even mind the fear.

He raced over the gorge, suppressing the urge to whoop and hold his arms out as wind whipped past him, blocking out any other sound. The ride lasted mere seconds, and then he was on the other side, his feet skidding over rock as he stumbled to a halt.

Grinning, he removed his gear, hoping Bethany got past her fear long enough to enjoy the experience. Training his binoculars on her, he watched her attach the rollers and harness, prepared to yank the line to get her attention if she got it wrong.

She didn't. Balancing on the tip of her toes, she swayed in the harness. He saw her mouthing a familiar chant in any language.

One. Two. Three.

She launched.

Good for her. She'd done the hardest part—jumping into the abyss. He kept the binoculars trained on her as she flew across the gorge, her eyes squeezed tight. He chuckled.

The squeal of metal against wood sounded behind him. The chuckle died on his lips. Whirling around, he watched as the barb started to pull free from the wood that held it.

A centimeter. Then two.

He grabbed the rope and pulled, trying to take some of her weight off the loosening barb then flicked his attention back to Bethany. Fifty feet from the edge, she slowed as the rope grew slack. Then stopped.

Son of a bitch. He pulled harder.

She opened her eyes, locking them on his. "Xavier?"

"Crank it!"

Her hands remained wrapped around the strap that held her to the rollers.

Despite his help, the barb squeaked again. He didn't dare look back to see how much was still in the tree.

"Do it," he shouted.

Her eyes slipped to where he strained to hold the rope.

"Hurry!"

Shaking, she reached for the crank and turned it. Once. Twice. She moved forward a foot.

"Keep going," he shouted. "You're doing great."

Her eyes returned to his. She gave another turn. Then another.

The rope dug into his palms. He grimaced, knowing he couldn't hold it much longer, and if the barb pulled free, they both were dead. She'd fall to her death, and he'd follow when the barb embedded itself in his hand and pulled him after her.

There was no way he was letting go. He was not going to lose her.

He gritted his teeth and pulled harder, the thought of Bethany falling to her death an almost unbearable torture.

Still dangling, she pulled her body weight forward. Her forehead glistened with sweat, the muscles in her arm quivered, but her eyes no longer sparkled with fear.

Determination had taken its place.

Ten feet left. "Come on, baby," he said through gritted teeth. "You can do it."

She didn't acknowledge him but moved forward, her focus on the roller above her. Seconds later, her feet landed on the edge of the gorge. The rope went slack in his hands. She took a step forward.

He'd almost lost her. Hands shaking, Xavier let go of the rope and unhooked her from the rollers.

She fell to her knees. "Let's never do that again," she said, her breathing ragged.

He fell beside her. Wrapping his arms around her, he pulled her to his chest. Thank God she was safe. But still, he shook at the thought he'd almost lost her.

And that scared him more than anything.

Still trembling against Xavier, Bethany looked over his shoulder. The barb that held her lifeline to the tree had managed to pull itself halfway out of the bark. "I could have died," she whispered. "Do you see that?"

"I do," Xavier said. He kissed the top of her head. "We'll stop here for the night."

"Now?" There was two hours' worth of light left. Despite being shaken, she wanted to hike. Adrenaline shivered through her, making her skin prickle and demanding she work off the excess energy.

"By the time we arrive, it'll be dark," Xavier explained. "I'd rather stay here and reach the camp in daylight. It makes everything easier." He kissed the top of her head again. "And I don't know about you, but I need a drink."

"We have alcohol?"

"Mescal. It makes a cheap disinfectant. Or can help on days like these."

Bethany nodded. She wasn't much of a drinker, but maybe it would stop the shaking. "Sounds good."

"I'll get it," Xavier said. He kissed her hair for a third time but instead of getting up to find the mescal, he bunched his hands in her hair, tilted her face to his and kissed her. Gentle at first, the kiss became fierce and demanding within seconds.

Who needed mescal and a walk? Xavier held her bottom lip between his teeth, and for a moment, she forgot to breathe. Breaking the kiss, she kissed a path to his shoulder, tasting the salt of his skin.

He unhooked her backpack. She let it fall backward and then slid her hand under Xavier's shirt.

"Bethany." He whispered her name and bit her neck hard enough to bruise.

It wasn't enough. She needed more. Needed Xavier to keep her grounded. "I need you," she whispered.

Groaning, he lay down on the bare stone, taking her with him then rolling over so she was beneath him and so close to the edge of the gorge that the breeze tossed her now-loose hair.

"You are magnificent," he mumbled. Hands shaking, Xavier unzipped her pants and his own, yanking them down as far as he was able.

Retrieving a condom, he slid it over his erection and in seconds, he was in her. Bethany arched upward. "More."

Xavier held her hips and thrust harder.

A climax rolled through her, and Bethany pulled Xavier to her, keeping him close as she arched beneath him. And in the back of her mind, she heard his cry.

When she opened her eyes, there was nothing but sky and trees above her. And Xavier.

He traced a path up her arm with his fingertips, and a sigh escaped her lips. "Did I hurt you?" he asked. "That was somewhat…"

"Intense?"

She caught his nod out of the corner of her eye. "I'm fine," she answered, loving that he had asked.

His fingers found their way to her torso then his hand flattened out, and he rested his palm on her stomach. "Then why are you crying?"

Bethany put a hand to her cheek and found it wet with tears. She'd never had that happen before. "I don't know," she replied. "Just happy to be alive, I guess."

"You cheated death. Tears are not an uncommon reaction." He leaned over her and kissed the corner of her mouth.

He was beautiful, she realized. He was everything she ever wanted—inside and out. She brushed his hair back, and he captured her hand and kissed her knuckles. "Rest. I'll make camp."

He wanted to treat her like a girl? This time, she wasn't going to object. "Thanks."

Letting the breeze that rose from the gorge cool her, Bethany closed her eyes and listened as Xavier pitched the tent and unpacked the minimum amount of gear needed for the night.

She knew the reason for her tears. It had nothing to do with cheating death and everything to do with Xavier. She had to tell him what she'd done. The lies. The money. *Everything.*

He wouldn't abandon her. He wasn't that kind of man.

But what was he going to do when he found out what kind of woman he'd agreed to assist? The kind of woman he'd made love to? He'd hate her.

And forgiveness? That was for someone else.

You're doing this for Samantha, a voice whispered. For your mother.

The rationalization didn't make her feel better.

Another tear slid down her cheek, and she wiped it away before he saw it.

Chapter 10

For what seemed like the hundredth time the next morning, Bethany tried to force herself to tell Xavier what she'd done. Last night, she'd lain awake long after he'd fallen asleep, rehearsing the words in her head. But no matter how she rearranged them, she still sounded like a liar.

That's because you are a liar.

That singular fact kept her silent. She was almost positive that despite her own lies, Xavier would keep his promise to save her sister.

It was who he was. What he did. Xavier wouldn't let her or Samantha down, despite her own transgressions.

But almost positive wasn't the same as completely positive, and the thought of taking a chance with Samantha's freedom— even a small chance—made her nauseous.

"Here." Xavier pointed her towards a wide path. "We're close."

Besides, he'd changed over the course of their morning trek. When she'd woken in his arms, he'd smiled at her, held her, stroked her skin and kissed her neck.

That Xavier was still at the edge of the gorge. The man leading her to FARC was harder. His heart held no pity or mercy. There was nothing of the Xavier from last night, she realized. This man was a soldier. A man who took money in exchange for his ability to take a life if necessary.

"How close?" Her voice squeaked. There was no way she was telling him the truth. Not now. She hoped to hell it was the right decision.

He cocked his weapon. "Close enough that we're going in locked and loaded. You fire on my signal. Not before." He made a gun barrel with his first two fingers and thumb to show her the move. "Is that clear?"

For a moment, she caught a glimpse of the Xavier from last night behind the black eyes and his worry for her. Then he was gone. She cocked her gun, as well. "I understand."

"Good, now stay behind me. We don't know—" He held up his hand, signaling silence.

"What is it?" she whispered.

He glared at her and held a finger to his lips. Then she heard it—conversation in Spanish farther up the trail and coming closer.

Xavier pushed Bethany away from the path and into a thick bush. Thirty feet in, he grabbed her hand, yanking her to the ground. She spit moss from her mouth and shook the dirt off her weapon. This was getting old.

The voices grew closer. Sweat broke out on her forehead. Had the men heard her and Xavier as they crashed into the jungle? If they hadn't, then they were either deaf or stupid. She glanced at Xavier. Crouched next to her, he still held his gun in one hand but in the other was a knife. Not large but large enough, sharp and silent enough to kill if they were discovered.

The blade gleamed in the shadows. She prayed it didn't come to that.

The voices continued, but the men stopped moving. Bethany strained to hear them as they spoke then rolled her eyes at her idiocy. Like that was going to help.

She promised that when she got out of this and was safe at home with Samantha, she'd learn Spanish.

Someone whacked at the foliage, confirming her fear. Bethany held her breath, positive they'd hear her if she so much as exhaled.

Something tickled her free hand. Bethany glanced down and caught herself before a shriek ripped through her throat. A snake—its brownish-orange scales broken up by a black stripe down the spine that also marked its sides like a tiger's stripes— slithered from behind her and glided across her hand on its way to who knew where. She swallowed hard and managed to hold herself still despite the singular, almost overwhelming urge to yank her hand away.

The snake paused, and she swallowed again. It's not poison- ous, she told herself, trying not to focus on the triangular- shaped head that was indicative of the viper family.

It's not poisonous.

She looked at Xavier. His eyes were huge.

Damn, she wanted to be right. Whatever the brand of snake crawling over her, it was very much poisonous.

Fifteen feet away, the FARC soldiers beat the leaves around them. The snake froze.

Oh, hell. This was going to get awkward, bloody and maybe lethal if something didn't happen soon. She looked at Xavier again.

Don't move, he mouthed.

As if she needed to be told.

The soldiers grew closer, and the snake twitched. She may not know what kind of snake it was, but she knew that if it bit her, she was screwed.

Xavier set his knife on the ground, taking care not to startle the snake any further. With his hand free, he grabbed the reptile at the back of the head. It thrashed for less than a second before he tossed it overhand toward the soldiers.

Through a gap in the leaves, Bethany watched the snake glide through the air, twisting, turning and coming to land on one of the soldiers.

He screamed and did a hyper little dance as he grabbed the snake and tossed it away then opened fire on the canopy above them, destroying leaves with a barrage of bullets.

She hugged the ground, covered her head with her arms and prayed that a stray bullet didn't hit her or Xavier by accident.

The shots stopped and shouting took its place. Nothing she understood but an angry tone that translated in any language. Cautiously, she raised her head.

From what she observed, neither man was hurt, but one was scared and from the gesturing and frowning, the other didn't think much of his fear.

They were both cowards as far as she was concerned.

The voices continued to argue then fade as the men continued down the trail.

They'd done it. No, she corrected herself—Xavier did it. He was creative and cool in a bad situation, and that was why she needed him. The fact he was hot and knew how to touch her in all of the right places was icing.

Delicious, wonderful icing.

Stop it, Bethany. Now is not the time.

She started to rise, and Xavier shook his head and held up five fingers.

Five minutes.

She nodded and relaxed. She'd come this far. She wasn't going to let impatience make her screw up.

He motioned for her to rise.

"That way," Xavier said, heading in the direction the men

had come from. They made their way, pushing through the jungle, staying silent and off the path. She tilted her head and noticed myriad sounds that didn't belong in the jungle. Metal on metal. Gravel crunching underfoot. And voices.

The camp. And it sounded as if it were over the rise in front of them.

Bethany dropped to the jungle floor before Xavier dragged her himself. He lay beside her and pointed forward with two fingers.

Worming her way to the top of the rise, she pushed the leaves apart.

The FARC encampment lay below them in the cleared-out hollow of the mountains. On the far side of the compound was a garden. A collection of scattered huts constructed of thick sticks that made it seem like a village built by the three little pigs—if the three little pigs had kept hostages.

One structure stood out. Covered with netting, she guessed it held weapons of some kind. Maybe food? There was no way to tell, and it didn't matter. She was here for Samantha. Nothing else mattered.

Feeling for the backpack behind her, she unzipped the side pocket in her pack and pulled out a pair of binoculars to survey the scene in more detail.

She'd read once that FARC was fueled by peasants. People tired of a repressive government. Men and women who wanted better than the government would offer.

The people below were dressed in rags, confirming her information. But she still found no pity in her heart. They might be peasants, but their guns were shiny and new, and if they once fought for a new government, that was a lot of idealism ago. Now they fought for the cocaine trade and a bigger bank account.

And they used hostages like her sister to do it.

If it were up to her, she'd gun them all down. She blinked hard, the blood-thirsty urge taking her by surprise.

Xavier's tap on the top of her hand brought her back to reality. She realized her hand was on the butt of her gun.

He shook his head.

She nodded. *Time to get a grip, Bethany.* Her heart pounding with hope, she scanned the faces below her. A few hostages worked in the garden. One lay on his side, chained to a tree.

All appeared gaunt and frightened. As if they spent every minute of every day—awake and asleep—walking on metaphorical eggshells.

But none of them were Samantha. She turned her focus to the huts. The stick sideing left gaps as wide as her hand, giving her a clear view of movement and shadow inside the huts, but she saw neither. The huts appeared empty. No doubt their occupants were toiling in the garden.

She zeroed in on the area. Again, her sister was nowhere in sight. "Where is she?" she whispered.

Xavier again shook his head.

Bethany's chest tightened, and she swallowed back the cry that tried to force its way from her throat. Samantha had to be here. Somewhere. She wasn't wrong.

But even as she tried to convince herself that she hadn't failed Samantha, guilt crashed over Bethany.

Time stopped as the world around her faded away. Her eyes squeezed tight and she fought to control her emotions. Instead, tears rolled down her cheeks as she gave in to doubt.

How was she going to tell her mother that her youngest daughter wasn't coming home? How was she going to look at herself in the mirror, knowing she was free while her sister walked the jungles of Colombia, treated worse than a dog?

And Xavier? Saving her sister had made the deception tolerable. Made the fact that he was going to wish her dead something she could live with.

Now, she didn't even have that. It wasn't fair. It just wasn't fair.

Something jabbed her in the lower back, and she recognized it as the wrong end of a weapon. She couldn't muster up the emotion to care. Not anymore.

"*Ese*, what kept you?" A familiar voice asked.

Sebastian. She smiled despite the tears. He was a goof, but he was good.

"Long story," Xavier said.

Bethany looked over her shoulder. Their two teammates hunkered down at her and Xavier's feet. "Hey, glad you could make it," she greeted, trying to smile and yet sure it looked like anything but a smile.

"*Chica*, what's wrong?" Sebastian asked though he looked to Xavier for an answer.

"We don't see Samantha," Xavier replied. She didn't miss the disappointment reflected in his voice, and it hurt her heart.

Tomas patted Bethany's calf. "She is on the far side of that little hill. In the good hut. We were just there."

Bethany stared at the men, her thought process hiccupping as she tried to go from despair to success in less than a second. "Are you sure?" She wasn't able to take another let down.

"You showed us her picture," Sebastian stressed, a hint of defensiveness in his tone.

"It is her, Bethany," Tomas replied, peeling her fingers from his arm. "We know our business."

"Show us," Xavier ordered.

"This way," Tomas said. All four backed up until they were able to rise to a crouching position without disturbing too much foliage. Tomas motioned for them to follow.

They made their way around the camp, taking care to avoid the occasional sentry and staying far enough in the foliage to remain unseen.

Had Tomas and Sebastian really seen her sister? She didn't want to hope and didn't dare to believe. When she hadn't seen

Samantha, it had almost killed her to think she'd failed both her sister and mother. A second time might just do her in.

They stopped at a large nut tree still in bloom, and Tomas motioned for them to move toward the camp. They worked their way in, stopping when they came to the edge of the clearing.

Sebastian pointed to a hut fifty feet away. Constructed of planed boards instead of the sticks that made up the other structures, it sat away from the rest of the camp like a throne before the peasants.

Come on. Bethany pulled out her binoculars. *Come on. Show me Samantha.*

Below them, there was movement. A man emerged from one of the ratty structures carrying a video camera. He wore camouflage cargo pants and a green sleeveless shirt. His head was shaved clean.

Her hands shook. Was it Cesar? If he was here, then Samantha was, as well. She zoomed in on his shoulder. A FARC tattoo stained the skin. Her hands shook harder.

He turned, facing her direction.

Cesar. The man from the videos.

Once again, she found her hand on her weapon.

Xavier put his hand on top of hers. "I know," he whispered.

She nodded, took a deep breath and relaxed. Later, she promised. She wanted Cesar dead, but first, she wanted him to suffer. She wanted him to lose what he valued most—money.

For some, death was just too easy a punishment.

A wicked smile curved her mouth upward. She was beginning to understand why Xavier saved hostages. It wasn't just for the families. It was to stab FARC and hurt them where it hurt the most.

In the wallet.

She focused her attention on Cesar's hut. "Come on, Samantha," she whispered. "Show me you're there."

"Quiet," Xavier whispered.

She realized they weren't alone. A man walked the perimeter one solid foot in front of the other. Bethany stilled, praying that the foliage over them was enough to hide them. He stopped a few feet from the small group and lit a cigarette, not bothering to look down.

Moron. She hoped all were as complacent. Though, even if they were, getting her sister out wasn't going to be as easy as she had hoped. There were a lot of men and a lot of guns.

Of course, she needed to see Samantha first, she reminded herself, reining in the rising hope. Confirm that the woman Sebastian and Tomas spotted was her sister.

Shouting broke out in the camp.

Xavier tapped her shoulder, gesturing for her to watch below. The sentry dropped his cigarette to the ground and without bothering to snuff it out, he sauntered down the hill.

Bethany put the binoculars up to her eyes and watched as Cesar stalked back toward the hut, hands gesturing. Two men emerged from the hut with someone between them. They pushed the prisoner forward. It was a woman, her hair and skin turned a muddy brown by the sun, a thick chain link wrapped around her neck and clothes so worn that charity would burn them.

Despite that, Bethany recognized the tilt of her chin. The green eyes that flashed anger.

Samantha.

The lenses blurred, but she didn't pull them away. Two years. Two years in hell, and there she was—her baby sister.

Bethany clenched her free hand into a tight fist, desperate to keep still and maintain position when every part of her wanted to run down the hill and throw her arms around Samantha. To pull her close and let her know she was safe now. That her big sister was here, and no one would ever hurt her again.

Xavier put his hand over hers. *Soon,* he mouthed.

Not soon enough, as far as Bethany was concerned. That would have been two years ago.

The FARC soldiers hauled Samantha to her feet then led her toward the garden with Cesar in the lead.

"She looks good," Xavier whispered.

"Good?"

"She is alive. Her feet aren't trashed. She can run. So yes, she looks good."

Bethany nodded. Perspective was everything. All she saw was her sister twenty or more pounds thinner with her hair chopped short.

But her eyes were still bright. Somewhere beyond the pain and fear, her Samantha was still there. "Okay, she looks good, but she's surrounded by a lot of bad men."

"Not too many and not too bad," Xavier observed.

"You have got to be kidding," Bethany whispered. "We're outnumbered and not just by one or two people. There are at least twenty FARC soldiers down there."

"You want to back out?" Xavier asked.

He wished.

This was it—Samantha's rescue. Her sister's salvation. And hers as well. Nothing was going to stop her now. "It could be the entire FARC militia down there and I'd still go."

"I am not comfortable with her going in," Sebastian offered, keeping to Spanish in front of Bethany as he unloaded one of the backpacks.

"Me, neither. But she hasn't made it easy to do otherwise," Xavier informed. They'd hiked an hour away from the camp. There would be no fire tonight—just planning, prep work and then back to the camp to take position before they slept.

Tomorrow was game time.

"There is always rope," Sebastian said, holding up a short length.

Xavier chuckled. He'd thought the same thing himself more than once. "Too dangerous."

"Afraid we'll get caught and she'll be left helpless?" Tomas guessed, without humor.

"No. Afraid we won't, and we'll have to bear her wrath," Xavier replied with all sincerity.

Sebastian chuckled, but Tomas nodded his head in understanding. Xavier smiled. His two teammates were night versus day in personality, but it was good to have both on the mission. They provided balance.

"Are you three talking about me?" Bethany inquired. "I have already told you, I'm not dumb. I know when I'm the topic."

"Excuse us," Sebastian apologized, switching back to the language they all understood. "It was not about you. We forget sometimes."

"Of course," she quipped, one eyebrow up in suspicion. Instead of challenging them, she sat on a fallen branch, the contents of her pack in neat piles around her feet.

Xavier feigned shock when she didn't pursue the issue. Bethany wasn't one to let anything go, but he was sure that thoughts of her sister made everything else seem less important.

Not that he blamed her. Seeing Samantha with a chain around her neck and being treated like a slave must have shocked her.

He prayed Eva received better treatment but knew that even prayer wouldn't make that wish come true.

How did the FARC soldiers sleep at night? he wondered for the millionth time. How did they take away another's freedom and look in the mirror and see a good person?

"So, what's next?" Bethany asked.

"Strategy," Xavier declared, refocusing on the task at hand. "And a little education."

"Education?"

"Tactical signals. Some lingo. The plan of attack. Who does what if we're discovered."

She straightened. "Teach me."

Ten minutes later, she knew as much as his men when it came to using tactical hand signals. Most were basic and almost international. A hand shading the eyes for *look* or a flattened hand outstretched for *stop*.

Some were not so common. A fist held up for *freeze*. An arm pump for *hurry up*. Circling the wrist with thumb and forefinger for *enemy*.

But she was quick.

She'd need that.

"Next, we have gear," Xavier continued, opening his pack.

"She'll be a pro by the time we are done," Sebastian announced, clapping Bethany on the shoulder. "We'll have to take her on more missions."

Xavier froze, his hand clutching one of the earpieces. The thought of Bethany going on more missions and putting herself in harm's way made his blood run cold.

He reminded himself that Sebastian was joking. Everyone dealt with stress in their own way, and his was by making light of the situation.

He took out the earpiece and tossed it to Sebastian. "Make yourself useful and teach her how this works."

He watched while Sebastian fitted the device on Bethany, showing her what buttons to push. He prayed they weren't doing the wrong thing by taking her.

No, not *them*. Not Sebastian and Tomas.

Him. He ran a hand through his hair. This was all about him and his family.

It's the right thing. It has to be.

But was it? Or is that what he needed to believe so he could sleep with a clear conscience?

"Xavier, she's good to go," Sebastian declared, tossing him an earpiece.

Xavier caught it in midair.

"How about the rest of the gear?" Bethany asked, leaning forward and pulling out a stick of dynamite. "Explosives? Flares? There's a lot in there for a girl to learn, and why don't I have any of that?"

Xavier took the dynamite from her hands and put it back in the pack. He didn't doubt Bethany's capabilities. He'd seen her under stress, and she handled it well. But this wasn't a panther encounter or crossing a gorge.

This was battle. A war. *Mano a mano,* as it were. If FARC fired at them, all bets were off as to what Bethany's reaction might be. Would she be able to handle explosives or would she be too scared to react?

The most common reaction was to either freeze or run. Freezing would be a problem. Running was worse.

He didn't mind her sprinting out as long as it was to safety. But if she were in flight mode, then she'd be running like a frightened animal, and frightened animals ran into things.

Like FARC troops.

So, it was up to him to make sure that scenario never happened. That there would be no gunfire in Bethany's direction and that she remained safe.

He zipped the pack shut. "Let's leave the high-powered stuff for people who have the experience."

"Xavier, I can do this."

He wasn't going to argue. Not about this. Instead, he cleared a spot on the ground. Picking up a stick, Xavier drew a crude map of the camp.

"This is Samantha." He made an *X* on the hut. He drew four more *X*s. Two above the camp. Two on the other side. Rectangles for the garden.

He tapped the two *X*s closest to the hut. "This is myself and Bethany." The three leaned in, focused on the mission, and he sent a prayer skyward that it went as planned.

Chapter 11

Xavier shook Bethany's shoulder, waking her, and she rubbed the sleep from her eyes. Last night, they'd returned to the FARC encampment at dusk, or as Sebastian liked to call it, "feeding time."

Funny man.

After helping her apply camouflage makeup and tucking her hair into a hat, Sebastian and Tomas had taken position on higher ground, ready to back them up and use cover fire if needed.

She hoped to hell that didn't happen.

Then she and Xavier took the closer location per plan, watching as the hostages were fed a dinner of what looked like watery beans and hard bread.

Bethany kept her attention on Samantha. Her sister didn't frown or push the food away but ate with a ravenous devotion and then licked the bowl.

Bethany promised herself that she'd buy Samantha whatever she wanted—pizza—once they were safe.

As far as she could tell, not a single prisoner said a word during the entire meal. Afterward, they were taken to the stick huts—one to a hut.

They're trying to break them, Bethany had realized, as night descended and the bugs came out. FARC forced the hostages into utter solitude without even communication to give them hope.

But that was eight hours ago. Now, night was changing to day and the jungle was coming to life around them. Monkeys screamed and chattered, and the cacophony of birds would mask some of the noise she and Xavier might make. The air was thick with the scent of decay mixed with the human scents of cooking from the camp below.

It was time to get her sister out. No more crappy beans. No more silence. Xavier tapped her and pointed toward Samantha's hut, his eyes questioning.

She nodded agreement.

"Blue team, what's our status?" Xavier whispered into his earpiece.

"Good to go. No players in sight. The lazy jerks," Sebastian replied.

That was what they'd been counting on—that the FARC soldiers would be either asleep or at the low point of their attention span.

"Heading in now," Xavier said.

Keeping low, Xavier headed toward Samantha's hut and motioned for Bethany to follow. Bethany took a deep breath and stepped out of the safety of the jungle. Below, there were two huts between themselves and the shack where Samantha was kept. One was the netted hut. The other held FARC.

Xavier made a controlled roll down the hill and landed on his feet.

Well, it was faster than walking and speed was essential. Bethany followed suit, tumbling down the slope and wishing for the cushy detritus of the jungle floor before landing on her side.

Before she could blink, Xavier grabbed her arm and she was on her feet, following him. They reached the far side of the net-covered hut and pressed themselves flat against the wall.

"Still good to go," Sebastian said.

"Gracias," Xavier whispered.

"De nada." They made it sound so casual. So easy. "Bethany, you're quiet. For a change," Sebastian teased.

"Butterflies," she muttered.

"Cut the chatter," Xavier said.

"Right, boss," Sebastian mocked. Bethany didn't miss the chuckle in his voice. Xavier edged around the corner of the hut, one hand behind him, palm out in a gesture that most of the world recognized as "talk to the hand." For her, it meant to *stop and wait*.

She took a deep breath to calm her racing heart. She'd done some daring things as a guide and in life. Shot the rapids of a Class 5 river. Hiked canyons untouched by man. And the zip-line…she'd never forget that.

But that was daring nature. People were different and even less predictable. Plus, they carried weapons. The more she thought about getting a bullet in the back, the more her hands shook.

Instead, she focused on what would happen after they rescued Samantha. The homecoming. The smile on her mother's face.

The anticipation pushed back the fear and she was ready.

Xavier lowered his hand then pumped it in the air, the signal for her to hurry up.

There was no need to tell her twice.

Xavier stepped out into the open and Bethany followed, keeping her eyes on the hut that held her sister.

Twenty steps and they were at the corner of the FARC hut. It was constructed better than the stick huts that held the hostages so she and Xavier wouldn't be seen, but any noise, any inkling that they were there, would get them killed or captured.

Another twenty steps and they were past the soldiers and heading toward Samantha.

They stopped at the door. Bethany took a deep breath. Xavier would go in first as discussed. She'd count to three and follow.

Unlatching the door, Xavier stepped inside.

One. It had been two years. Would Samantha instantly recognize her? Bethany clenched and unclenched her hands.

Two. Would Samantha forgive her?

Three. One way or another, it was time to find out.

She stepped through the door and froze. Samantha was awake, aware and pressed against the wall with Xavier's hand over her mouth.

The need to protect her sister was sudden and intense and rocked her to the bone. Bethany crossed the small hut in two steps. "What are you doing?" she asked. Her hand out to grab Xavier's away from Samantha's mouth, she stopped just short.

If it were anyone else…

"She doesn't know me," Xavier explained. "She tried to scream. So unless you want us all dead, talk her down."

Samantha looked at her, green eyes wide. No, not at her, Bethany realized. Through her. What the hell had FARC done to her?

"Sweetie, it's Bethany." She touched her sister's hair, and Samantha flinched, squeezing her eyes shut. Bethany took off her hat to show her hair and used the cloth to wipe her face. "It's just makeup. This is Xavier Monero." She tapped Xavier's arm. "We're here to take you home."

Samantha inched her eyes open and then relaxed in Xavier's arms. He removed his hand but kept it ready in case Samantha tried to shout.

"Bethany?" she whispered. Her voice sounded lower. Hoarse.

Still, Bethany recognized it and hearing her sister brought tears to her eyes. Bethany nodded and brushed her hand against Samantha's cheek. "It's me."

Samantha leaned into her touch with a sigh. "I knew you'd come."

Bethany smiled. She didn't deserve such trust. She wrapped her arms around her sister's shoulder and pulled her close. Bethany felt her ribs beneath the torn rag of the shirt Samantha wore and eased her hug, afraid she'd snap a bone or bruise her.

"Save the reunion," Xavier interrupted, clapping a hand on Bethany's shoulder. "We need to leave."

Bethany tore herself from Samantha. "Can you walk?"

"I'd run on broken glass if it meant getting out of here," Samantha responded.

"Do you have anything for your feet?" Xavier asked.

"Rags."

"It'll do. Hurry."

Samantha grabbed a wad of cloth scraps. Dirty and smelling of old sweat, Bethany tried not to flinch as she helped Samantha wind them around her feet. "When we get back, I'm getting you some proper shoes," she whispered.

"I'd settle for a shower."

"That, too."

"Red team, we have a player in motion." Sebastian's voice came over the earpiece and Bethany stilled.

"What's wrong?" Samantha asked, her voice trembled.

Xavier held up his hand, asking for silence. "Location?"

"Headed toward the camouflaged structure. Orders?" Sebastian answered.

"Stay put. We give two minutes. If he's still there, I'll take care of it."

"Counting," Sebastian indicated.

Xavier glanced at his watch.

"Do we have two minutes?" Bethany finished wrapping Samantha's foot and waited while her sister wrapped the other.

"I'd rather not have to run for it. If we can get out unobserved, it'll be better for everyone."

"I waited two years. I can wait a little longer," Samantha said.

She grabbed Bethany's hand, and Bethany squeezed her tight. Samantha's nails were short and broken. A far cry from the woman who considered a mani-pedi a weekly "must do." She'd buy her a lifetime's worth once she was safe.

"I never doubted you'd come for me," Samantha whispered. "Even when they told me about the money."

Bethany tightened. No. No. No. Not here.

Xavier cocked his head. "What about the money?"

"It's nothing," Bethany claimed, swallowing hard.

"It's everything." Samantha's green eyes met Xavier's. "They refused to settle for less than half a million and Bethany didn't have close to that."

Xavier looked at Bethany. Disbelief in his eyes.

She opened her mouth but nothing came out. She wanted Xavier to know the truth. He deserved the truth, but not here and not from her sister. Neither could she tell her sister to shut the hell up.

Bethany glanced at her watch. A minute to go. Crap.

"How much did she have?" Xavier asked.

"I don't know," Samantha said. "But it didn't matter. She came for me. I knew she wouldn't leave me here."

"It matters to me." Xavier's gaze bored into Bethany.

Bethany worried her lower lip as her gaze flickered between Xavier and Samantha. There was no running away from the truth now. Location and timing be damned, he wouldn't let it go. He simply wasn't that type of man.

Taking a deep breath, she braced herself for his anger. "I don't have the money," she whispered. "I never did."

For a beat Xavier stared at her, but there was no anger in his eyes. There was a flash of disbelief and disappointment and then, nothing.

Cold, cold nothing.

She knew that's what she was to him now. *Nothing.*

And the pain of losing Xavier almost drove her to her knees. Shaking, Bethany prayed that she could make him understand that she had no choice. That she didn't mean to hurt him or Eva. And, while she might have lied about the cash, what she felt for him was real.

"Um, what's going on?" Samantha asked. "Is there a problem?"

Bethany pressed her lips tight at hearing the fear in her sister's voice. As much as she wanted to explain her actions, Sam had already been through enough, and she would not burden her sister any more than necessary.

Not now. Not when they were all so close to success.

Her apology and explanation would have to wait.

She turned to Samantha. "Everything is fine, but we should be quiet," she said. "There'll be time to talk later. Once we have you safe. Right now, we need to focus."

"Of course," Samantha said, squeezing her hand again. "I want to hear everything. About Mom. Your life. Everything."

Their mother. Another sensitive subject and one best left for when she could tell Samantha the entire story. "You will. I promise."

Bethany snuck a peek at Xavier. He watched the entrance, waiting for word from Sebastian as to their next move.

He glanced over his shoulder, his eyes meeting hers.

There was more than anger there. There was a fury so deep and dark it cut her all the way to her core. He turned back to the door, and it took everything in her not to reach out to him.

Instead, she focused on the warmth of her sister's hand in hers. Two years of worry and waiting were over.

Let him be angry. Holding Samantha's hand in hers was worth the price of his wrath.

Xavier glanced at his watch. Ten seconds and he'd go take care of the problem of the player. A part of him hoped the FARC soldier stayed put. A stupid wish, but the desire to do something destructive was undeniable, and as angry as he was with Bethany, he wasn't going to take it out on her sister.

He'd made a promise, after all, and he'd be damned if he was going to break it. Bethany might be a Judas but he wasn't.

He looked at the sisters. Samantha glowed with happiness. Not a shock considering the rescue. Bethany, when she looked at him, at least had the sense to show shame.

Good.

But when she looked at Samantha, her happiness at having her sister back overrode the lies. She was happy, and he hated her for that. Hated them both for having what he'd never have—a happy reunion.

Bethany had taken that from him.

Bitch.

He looked again at his watch.

Time's up.

He tapped his earpiece. "Status?"

"Still in play."

Most of all, he hated Bethany for putting himself and his men in this position. "I'll take care of it. Cover me."

"You got it."

"What are you going to do?" Bethany asked.

Unable to look at either sister, he holstered his weapon and pulled his knife from its sheath. "What I have to."

He edged the door open. It was as clear. "If it goes south, you do what Sebastian says. Do you understand?"

"We understand," Bethany said.

He slid out and closed the door behind him. Keeping low,

he pushed Bethany to the back of his mind and hurried toward the netted hut.

He stopped shy from entering and pressed himself against the wall, listening. There was rustling and the clink of metal on metal. Weapons? Readying the gear to move? Sorting cooking pots?

There was no way to tell.

What he needed to know was the man's position. Did he face the door or away from it? He looked for a gap on the boards that wasn't blocked by the boxes on the other side.

There wasn't anything, and the day grew brighter every minute.

He edged around to the door. There was the groan of hinges inside the hut but nothing more.

Knife in hand, Xavier opened the door and stepped inside. The FARC soldier stood at attention facing away from the door. In front of him was an open weapons box.

He'd called it right. It was good to see he hadn't lost all of his instincts.

In the time it took for the soldier to turn, Xavier crossed the span between them. The man opened his mouth to call for help and reached for a gun. Before he could do either, Xavier clamped a hand over his mouth and pushed his knife into the man's neck, slicing the carotid artery.

In seconds, he went limp and Xavier lowered him to the ground. "Damn," he whispered, closing his eyes. This wasn't a man. It was a boy with a sparse mustache and skin still red with teenage acne.

Young or not, he'd sided with FARC, and there were few happy endings for a FARC soldier.

Xavier tapped his earpiece. "Status?"

"No other players in sight," Sebastian said. "It's getting late. Time to move."

"Agreed."

"Bethany?"

"Here," she replied.

"I want you and Samantha to get to me. Sebastian will cover you."

"On our way."

Xavier frowned at hearing how normal her voice now sounded.

Standing by the door, he took a deep breath and tried to calm himself. Why did she do it? Why hadn't she told him the truth before it came to this? It wasn't as if she didn't have the opportunity.

The door to the hut opened, and the two women rushed in with Samantha in the lead. Both stopped mid step, their attention on the body and the blood that pooled around the dead man's head.

Clamping her hand over her mouth, Bethany turned away and tried to turn Samantha away as well, but her sister shook her off.

Xavier didn't miss the glint of satisfaction in the younger girl's eyes. He couldn't blame her gut reaction. This boy helped keep her captive.

To her, he'd received what he deserved.

But then, leaning over, Samantha placed her hands on her knees, and Xavier realized that she couldn't seem to catch her breath. He frowned. Her feet might be okay, but this wasn't about her feet. Samantha was sick. There was no doubt about that. "What's wrong?"

Samantha shook her head. "I'm not sure. Bronchitis, I think."

"She had asthma when she was young," Bethany relayed, her hand on her sister's shoulder. "Maybe it's come back."

"I wasn't asking you," Xavier snapped.

Samantha straightened, palms pressed against her lower back as her breathing calmed. "What's going on with you two?" she asked, looking at Xavier and then her sister.

"Nothing," Bethany replied.

Xavier tried not to sneer.

"It sounds like something," Samantha corrected. She tried to take another deep breath then bent over to muffle a cough.

"It's not," Bethany argued. "It's *nothing*. We need to hurry."

Nothing? Xavier stared at Bethany, willing her to feel his pain and admit her transgressions, but she looked anything but contrite and his anger at her betrayal spiraled. "It's not nothing. Eva is not nothing. What you did is not nothing."

Bethany paled at his disclosure, and a bitter satisfaction rushed through Xavier. Bitter or not, he embraced it.

"Who's Eva?" Samantha asked, head cocked.

"My sister," Xavier answered. "She is also a FARC hostage."

"Please." Bethany crossed her arms over her chest, begging him without words.

Xavier took a deep breath. As much as he wanted to hurt her, to make her feel his pain, he couldn't do it. Not again. He didn't take his eyes off Bethany. "Bethany was supposed to help me rescue her as well, and let's just say that isn't going to happen."

Thank you, she mouthed.

"Eva Monero," Samantha interrupted. "About my height? Has a tattoo of a broken heart on her left wrist?"

Xavier whirled to face Samantha. The tattoo was in memory of their brother, Miguel. "Yes," he replied, the words sticking in his throat. "You have seen her? Is she here?"

"I have," Samantha replied, dragging the words out. "She's not here. She's at the camp at the end of the gorge. A full day's walk up the path. Maybe a little more."

His anger towards Bethany fell away beneath the hope that surged through him. A day's hike was close enough for him to get to Eva and that was all he needed. Xavier grabbed Samantha's shoulders, already formulating a rescue plan. "When did you see her last? Is she okay?"

"A few days ago. She's fine." Samantha took a step back, out of his grasp. "But she's not a hostage. She's a member of FARC."

Bethany stared at her sister. Had she heard right or were the two years in captivity messing with her head, making her see and say things that weren't right? "What?"

"She's a member of FARC. She dropped off two prisoners just a few days ago."

"Liar." Xavier's forced the word through gritted teeth. "Just like your sister."

"Samantha doesn't lie," Bethany shot back, stepping between the two. "Say what you want about me, but Samantha has been through enough without hearing your accusations."

Xavier stared at Samantha, and Bethany wondered what was running through his head. Finally, he gave a curt nod. "That doesn't make her right."

Bethany frowned. "It doesn't make her wrong either. And I—"

"Are you three going to hang out there all morning?" Sebastian broke in on her headset, cutting her off. "Do you have a death wish?"

"Of course not," Xavier replied, without a hint of the anger from seconds ago. Now he was professional. All mercenary. "Status?" he asked Sebastian.

"Minute."

They waited.

"Hold position," Sebastian instructed. "We have a player. He's heading toward what looks like an outhouse."

Xavier gave Samantha a once over. "It isn't far to the bridge. Can you make it?"

Bethany knew what he was thinking—that she might be too weak to run. Samantha nodded. "What about the guards?"

Xavier held up his knife.

Samantha smiled, and for a heartbeat, Bethany saw bloodlust in her sister's eyes. Samantha liked the thought of her captors being killed. She wanted them dead.

Then the glimmer of hate faded as quickly as it had appeared, making Bethany wonder if it ever existed.

"What happens once we're over?" Samantha asked. "How do you plan to get out of here after the bridge? Jeep?"

"On foot," Bethany informed.

"Sounds great."

Now Samantha was a liar as well.

"What's to keep them from following us?" Samantha continued. "It won't take long for them to find out I'm gone."

Xavier responded. "Once we're over the bridge, we'll blow it."

"Good, that'll hurt them," Samantha remarked. Then her sister frowned. "But what about the others?"

"The other prisoners?" Bethany asked.

"My escaping is going to make it harder for them. If we blow the bridge, it'll make it worse."

"No choice," Xavier declared.

"He's inside." Sebastian's voice broke over the earpiece. "Get out. We're burning daylight."

Taking Samantha's arm, Xavier guided her to the door.

"Promise me you'll come back for them," Samantha insisted. She looked to Bethany. "Promise me."

"Get moving," Xavier ordered.

"Promise me."

Xavier didn't say a word.

Two years in captivity hadn't changed her sister's stubborn streak. But her bravery and compassion was unexpected. Bethany admired it, and it shamed her as well. "I promise," Bethany vowed.

"Him too."

Xavier clenched his jaw tight. "I promise. Can we go now?"

Bethany felt sorry for anyone that tried to stop him. He looked ready to cause damage. Opening the door, he pointed toward the top of the rise. "You're going that way. Keep to the trail and stay with Bethany. I'll be right behind you. Sebastian and Tomas will meet us at the bridge."

"I'll keep up," Samantha assured.

"Just go," Xavier growled.

Bethany grabbed her sister's hand again and pulled her into motion. Xavier ran as silent as a predator but his presence behind her, protecting them, was undeniable.

In seconds, they stood at the base of the hill they'd rolled down. She glanced at Samantha. Her sister was already breathing hard, but she'd get a chance to catch her breath once they were on the other side of the bridge.

Halfway up, Samantha's breathing rattled and she slowed.

Come on, Samantha. You can do this.

"Heads up," Sebastian's voice cut over the radio. "We got company."

Bethany pulled on Samantha, forcing her to move faster toward the tree line. Almost there.

Safety and freedom.

Samantha collapsed, slid two feet and came to a stop.

Chapter 12

Samantha! Bethany stopped, but before she could turn back, Xavier was by Samantha's side.

"Keep moving." He picked up her sister and continued to run up the hill. They were at the tree line when Bethany heard a shout from behind them.

She looked over her shoulder. Cesar stood in the doorway of Samantha's hut, his face twisted in anger, screaming orders and pointed toward the fleeing trio.

His eyes met hers just as she disappeared into the leaves, but she didn't smile. It was too early in the mission for that. Still, a sliver of satisfaction that wound around her like a blanket gave her strength.

"How is she?"

"Awake," Samantha answered. She wrapped her arms around Xavier's neck as she fought to catch her breath. "You can put me down."

"And have you faint again?" Xavier proposed. "Pass." He glared at Bethany, his anger not abated by the current dash for freedom. "Let's move."

They hustled through the jungle, no longer caring about noise. Let the animals wake. Let the birds scream. If they didn't make the bridge before FARC caught them, they were all screwed.

Despite the burden of carrying Samantha, Xavier kept pace next to her. He amazed her. He'd called Samantha a liar, yet he carried her to freedom because he'd made her a promise. He was everything she aspired to be. Honest. Strong. Brave. And she loved him for that.

Loved him?

Where did that come from? She almost stopped.

"Keep moving," Xavier spat, slowing to match her.

She picked up the pace. "What about the guards at the bridge?" she asked, jumping over a branch like a runner clearing a hurdle.

"Sebastian and Tomas will take care of that."

Good men loyal to a good man.

Behind them, crashing and shouting echoed through the jungle. Bethany didn't look back. In the jungle, it required less than ten yards to maintain invisibility, and they were at least fifty yards ahead of them, if not more.

Just stay ahead of FARC. That was all they needed.

The "pop pop" of gunfire behind them urged her to greater speeds, and seconds later, they stumbled into the path that led to the bridge. "Almost there," Xavier encouraged.

They crested the small incline in the trail, and the gorge opened before them with the bridge just ahead. Sebastian stood next to two bodies, and Tomas lay on his back, his hands busy beneath the slats of the bridge.

She couldn't see what he was doing, but she guessed he was setting the charges to take down the bridge. Made of wood and metal, it was wide enough to allow men and pack animals to pass but no more.

"Now can I get down?" Samantha asked.

Xavier set her on her feet, and she wavered for a moment. Sebastian grabbed her, one arm around her waist.

"*Hola, señorita.* You must be Samantha."

Bethany rolled her eyes. Half of FARC was after them and Sebastian still managed to make a simple hello sound like a pickup line.

"Yes," Samantha replied.

"Help her," Xavier said looking at Bethany. "You," he spoke while nodding to Sebastian. "Keep watch."

"*Sí.*"

"How's it going, Tomas?" Xavier prodded, watching the jungle, waiting for FARC to arrive. "We need to get those charges set before they arrive."

Tomas sat up. "All done. Let's go."

"How much time on the fuse?" Gunfire sounded from the jungle behind them.

"Sixty seconds," Tomas indicated, taking a lighter from a side pocket in his camouflage pants. "Enough for us to get across, but unless we want company on the other side, we need to go. Now."

"Take Samantha," he said to Tomas. "And you," he glared at Bethany. "We'll talk later. I promise."

Bethany's mouth went dry. "What's going on?"

"I'm staying behind."

He couldn't stay behind with a whole camp on their ass. "Are you crazy?"

"I'm going after Eva."

Both Sebastian and Tomas straightened at the news. "Eva is here?" Tomas asked.

"Up the gorge, according to *her.*" He shot Samantha a glance that told everyone she might be right or she might be nuts, but either way, Xavier was going to get to the truth. "I need you two to get these two to safety. FARC doesn't know how many people are here, and I don't want them to think anyone was left on this side." He held out his hand. "Lighter."

Tomas hesitated then handed him the lighter. "Bring it back. It belonged to my brother."

"You'll get it back," Xavier replied.

"I will stay," Sebastian offered. "You will need help."

Bethany shook her head. She'd done everything to save her sister and she was not going to compromise her safety. Not now. But neither was she going to let Xavier go alone, mercenary mode or not. "My sister needs you both to get her out. I'll stay."

"Like hell," Xavier cursed. "No one is staying."

She glared at him, her jaw tight. He might not want to admit it, but he needed someone to guard his back.

"You can't stop me," she countered, her voice calm. "Besides, I owe you. Time to pay up."

"You want to pay up? Then give me the half million dollars you promised me."

His words were as hard as a slap, and she flinched at their ferocity, but she refused to back down. She wasn't going to give him the satisfaction or the opportunity to sink further into the wounded mercenary role.

"It all comes down to Eva," she explained. "I'm going with you, and there is no time to argue."

"*Ese*, we have to go." Sebastian glanced the way they'd come.

Xavier hesitated for a heartbeat, his lips pressed tight. "Take Samantha. Bethany and I will catch up. Head for Veron's camp. He'll be pissed if he finds out the truth but you'll be protected."

Bethany wasn't sure if his agreement to let her go made her happy or ill. Her stomach did a slow roll.

Ill it was.

She wrapped her arms around Samantha and kissed her cheek.

"Be careful," Samantha whispered.

"I'll see you in a few days."

Samantha nodded, her eyes wet.

"You two," she demanded as she faced Sebastian and Tomas, "take care of my sister."

They hurried Samantha to the bridge, keeping her between them as they began the crossing.

"How good is his timing?" Bethany said, watching the three run across the span. It wouldn't take much of a miscalculation for the dynamite to blow with them on the bridge instead of safe on the other side.

"Tomas is the best," Xavier said. He flicked the lighter open, and a second later, the fuse hissed to life.

He let the lit line drop under the bridge and out of sight. "Move it."

She followed him along the edge of the gorge, forcing herself to gaze into its dizzying depths. She'd never liked heights, and now, she liked them even less.

"Stop here." Xavier halted thirty yards from the bridge.

"What are we waiting for?" Bethany asked.

"To make sure no one from FARC gets across."

"Is this far enough from the explosion?"

Xavier shrugged. "It never seems like far enough but any farther, and we'll lose the view."

FARC's shouts grew closer, and they knelt down, peeking at the scene through the vegetation. Sebastian, Tomas and Samantha were almost across.

Bethany bit her lower lip. She wouldn't feel good about this until they were on the other side. Safe.

Come on.

The FARC soldiers emerged from the jungle and ran onto the bridge. The structure dipped and shook with their weight.

It took all her discipline not to shout for the three to hurry the hell up. The sixty-second fuse felt like sixty years.

Samantha stumbled and almost fell. Bethany's breath caught

in her throat. Tomas scooped her up in his arms, and Bethany found the ability to breathe again.

Sebastian's feet hit the ground on the other side, and Tomas followed seconds later. He didn't set Samantha down. They disappeared into the jungle.

Get my sister home, boys.

"Look." Xavier glanced at his watch.

The FARC soldiers were on the bridge.

"Five. Four. Three," Xavier muttered the countdown.

They were almost halfway across and two more set foot on the bridge, as well.

"Two," Bethany joined in, putting her hands over her ears.

The terrorists would never know what hit them.

"One."

Nothing happened. Bethany stared, unable to believe they'd failed. That FARC was going to recapture her sister. "What's wrong—"

The bridge erupted. A pink spray tinted the air as the last two soldiers were caught in the blast. Chunks of wood flew through the air, and the steel cables holding the structure to the side of the gorge whipped free. The men in the middle of the bridge tumbled into the gorge, screaming.

Xavier watched the half dozen men fall to their deaths and felt no remorse. It was a crappy way to die but no less than the cowards deserved. Men who took hostages, especially women, didn't deserve to die in battle like a hero.

Still, there was no time to contemplate good and evil or honor and shame. He knew his sister's location, and with that knowledge, came hope.

Despite what Samantha thought she knew, Eva wasn't a terrorist. The girl was wrong, but it was to be expected. She'd been held prisoner. Who knew what was going through her head.

She'd need therapy for years, and though Bethany was

happy to have her back, he knew Samantha would never be the girl she remembered. She'd seen too much. Been through too much.

And he'd yelled at her. Called her a liar. Shame twisted through him. Later, he'd explain himself and perhaps apologize. Samantha deserved his sympathy, not his animosity.

"Now what?" Bethany whispered.

He glanced at the guide. Her sister might have a reason to deserve an apology. She didn't. "We leave before the others arrive." Xavier broke into a slow jog along the gorge. Samantha said the camp was just over a day's walk, but that was for hostages who were kept weak so they couldn't escape.

He and Bethany would need one day. Less if he pushed her. And he planned to push her hard.

"How long before they come after us?" Bethany asked as they ran.

"They won't."

"Why not?"

"Why would they think we stayed?" Xavier suggested. "You should stop talking. Conserve energy."

"I meant to tell you," she said.

"Meaning to and following through are two different things." What did she want from him? Absolution? She wasn't going to get it, and he didn't want to say any more. Her betrayal was too fresh and the pain too deep.

"Xavier?"

He didn't answer.

"Xavier," she called, again, this time more insistent.

Apparently, his silence wasn't enough to tell her to shut up. "I don't want to talk about this."

"We have to."

"No, we don't."

"We can't just *not* talk about it."

Xavier groaned. She was not going to let this go. Stubborn

pain-in-the-ass. "What is it you feel needs to be said?" He kept his pace. "You lied. End of story."

"I didn't know what else to do," Bethany explained.

"Telling the truth was an option."

"I didn't know you." She grabbed his forearm, and he shook her off.

Though she didn't say it, he heard the unspoken *I didn't trust you.* That burned the most.

She continued. "Can you say you'd have taken me on as a client if I told you I didn't have all the money?"

He liked to think he would have, but he knew the answer. "At first? No. But later? Perhaps. The point is, you took my choice away."

"I know. I know." Bethany scrubbed her face with a palm, smearing her remaining camouflage makeup into a muddy mess. "I was afraid."

"Of what? That I'd abandon you?"

"Yes."

His face warmed with renewed anger. Did she think him a monster? "Thanks."

"She's my sister, Xavier. I couldn't take that chance. Of all people, you should understand that."

He did, but that didn't make it any easier to hear. He'd been convinced that there was something between them. What, he wasn't sure, but it was something different. Something he'd never felt before.

Now he wondered if he'd been kidding himself. That he'd seen more because he wanted more. "What do you want from me, Bethany?"

"Forgiveness?"

He barked a laugh.

"I figured as much." She stopped, forcing him to do the same. Hands on her hips, she looked up at him in a way that had become familiar in just a few days.

And that fueled his anger. He didn't want familiarity. Not with her.

"Just think about it," Bethany suggested. "Promise me that you'll think about what I did and why and try to understand."

"I don't have to promise you anything." He looked her up and down. Beautiful, beautiful liar. "Let's move."

She crossed her arms over her chest. "I'm not taking another step until you promise."

He'd dealt with petulant children before and this was no different. One didn't give in to the tantrum. One walked away. "Have it your way." He headed up the gorge.

A few minutes later, she hurried to catch up. "This isn't over," she asserted.

Let her think what she wanted, but as far as he was concerned, it was over—they were over—the minute he'd found out the truth.

"We are so screwed," Bethany whispered.

She and Xavier lay on the ridge above the camp. The camp that had held Samantha was a quarter of the size of the one below them. Where they'd had burros and llamas, this one had jeeps.

And the soldiers at this camp paid attention. They even had a uniform, of sorts. Floppy camouflage hats and matching jackets over an army-green shirt. "There is no way we're going to sneak in there," Bethany concluded. "No way."

"There is always a way," Xavier proclaimed, scanning the camp, looking for Eva.

"If you say so," Bethany muttered, focused on looking for Xavier's sister. But there were few female soldiers, and Bethany didn't know what Eva looked like. Ten minutes later with no word from Xavier that he'd spotted her, Bethany wondered if Samantha was mistaken.

"Maybe we should go," Bethany whispered.

"No, she's here," Xavier said.

Bethany straightened. "What?"

"There." He pointed to a group of soccer players. "The girl. That's Eva."

How long had he been watching her? Bethany raised the binoculars. There was one girl in the group of ten men. Her long, black hair curled from the heat and her olive skin glowed from playing. She laughed and Bethany caught sight of a smile that belonged in an ad for toothpaste. "She's beautiful."

"And one of FARC," Xavier said. "Maybe."

His expression gave nothing away, but he couldn't hide the disappointment in his voice. Bethany knew there was nothing she could say to help. Nothing she could do to assuage his pain. But she tried anyway. "You know, it could be Stockholm syndrome. It makes the hostage sympathize with the kidnapper."

"I know what Stockholm syndrome is," Xavier snapped. "I need to talk to her."

Bethany's brow shot upward. She couldn't blame him, but getting to Eva was on a par with walking into the lion's den, and she couldn't see a scenario where that was a good idea. "How do you propose to do that? This place isn't like where they held Samantha. It might not have walls, but even I can see it's a fortress."

Xavier glanced over at her and set his binoculars on the ground. "Watch her. I need to know where she goes."

"Where are you going?" The sun would set soon, and the thought of being left alone in the jungle at night was almost more frightening than being on the perimeter of a FARC camp.

"To get something that'll help us." He walked into the jungle and disappeared within a few meters.

Bethany took a deep breath and returned her attention to Eva. What the hell was wrong with her? Why would anyone join FARC?

She was sure that Xavier would ask Eva the same thing.

She shuddered at the thought of the confrontation. That was going to be an ugly conversation.

Ten minutes later, Xavier stepped out of the leaves, startling her. "Where's Eva?"

Bethany jumped. "Are you trying to give me a heart attack?"

He didn't reply. No quip. No comeback. Just a cold, hard stare.

She turned back over. "Still playing soccer."

"Good. Keep an eye out." He tossed a FARC jacket and shirt on the ground next to her and began to strip.

"Where did you get those?" Bethany asked.

"Where do you think?" Xavier said, slipping the green shirt over his head. It stretched tight across his shoulders.

Bethany sat up. She knew what he was doing, and while she knew she couldn't talk him out of it, she could at least try to get him to approach it in a rational way. "You said that dusk was the worst time to do anything. That everyone would be bored and looking for trouble. We should wait until morning."

"There is no *we*. It's a large camp. No one will know who I am. Dusk will help shadow my features." He put on the jacket. The sleeves reached midforearm. Barely. He took it off and tossed it to the ground.

So, rational wasn't an option. Dammit, why did he have to be so pigheaded?

Pigheaded or not, she wasn't letting him go alone. Maybe there wasn't a "we" anymore, but she was still his partner, his teammate, and he was not going in there without her.

She picked up the jacket and slipped it on. A bit big but that was a good thing.

"What are you doing?" Xavier demanded. From his tone, he knew what she was doing and didn't sound too thrilled.

She didn't care. He could bitch and rant, but her mind was made up. "What does it look like?"

"You're not going."

Bethany looked up at him; the anger in his gaze was undeniable. She jerked away. "You'll need someone on your side down there, and right now, I'm it."

"I have Eva."

"You can't be sure of that," she clarified, not caring if the insinuation pissed him off. She wasn't too happy with this idea. Let him feel her anger, for once.

Xavier glared at her. "In case you didn't notice, there aren't many women there. You'll be noticed."

"There are enough." She buttoned the jacket all the way to her throat to cover her femininity. It smelled like sour sweat. "This helps."

"You stand out."

"It's dusk," she said, tossing his argument back at him.

"Not dusk enough."

He gazed at her, making her squirm under the scrutiny.

Bethany rested her head in her hands. She was tired of arguing and he might be angry with her, but she needed to make him see that Eva was FARC despite what she'd suggested earlier.

"You want me to stay behind? Then don't go." She raised her face to his. His expression was as unmoved. "You can see she's made her choice. Let's leave before another solider finds us."

He stared down at her, his mouth as solid and stern as stone. "I won't leave her here, alone, until I get the full story. From her."

Bethany sighed. As much as she hated to admit it, she'd do the same thing if their positions were switched. "Let's move out and get this over with."

His stony expression softened, and Xavier turned away.

Bethany waited. They both knew she wasn't a liability, but she sure as hell wasn't an asset. He didn't need her. Not for this.

But they also both knew that she wasn't going to remain behind. Not now.

And if she had her way, not ever.

Chapter 13

This is the worst idea ever. Or the best.

Bethany couldn't decide which as she followed Xavier, avoiding patrols and looking for a place to enter the camp with minimal issues.

Either way, his plan to walk in, acting as if they belonged, was audacious as hell. She hoped it was unconventional enough to work.

"Down," Xavier whispered. She ducked, and a minute later, a FARC soldier strode past them, unaware they lurked in the foliage just off the trail.

Still, a prickle of fear ran a hurried course up her spine.

Xavier tapped the top of her hand, held up one finger and pointed to the camp.

One minute and they were going in.

She gave a tight nod, eager to end the expedition. She glanced upward while time ticked in her head. It wasn't dark yet, but already a few stars decorated the purpling sky. She turned back toward the camp to listen for the sound of the game.

She caught laughter. Chatter. But it was too indistinct to know the source. Were they too late? If so, they'd have to wait until tomorrow and she couldn't see Xavier doing that. Nor could they go door-to-door and knock.

Xavier tapped her again. No more speculation.

Bethany swallowed hard. She thought crossing the gorge had been difficult. Sure, it scared the hell out of her, but it was predictable. Gravity pulled you down. Rock was harder than bone.

For every action there was an equal and opposite reaction.

All the laws of physics in one happy, logical bundle.

But people followed no such rules. They made decisions based on emotion, desire or need. Decisions like hers. Like Xavier's.

Damn, they were screwed if they were caught.

Screwed or not, she wasn't going to let Xavier down. Not again. She was going to prove to him that he could count on her. Stepping through the fronds and moss, she followed Xavier into the compound between two of the huts covered with camouflage netting.

Once again, goose bumps shivered up her spine. But no one called them out. There was no gun fire. No shout of alarm.

Success. So far. "Well, we're here. How do you plan to get to Eva?"

"Keep your head down. Walk fast. Follow my lead." Xavier checked his weapon. He didn't look angry. He looked worried.

But he also looked determined as hell.

"That's it?" It didn't sound like much of a plan and determination was little comfort when she thought about walking through a FARC encampment. "What do I do if someone speaks to me?"

He shrugged. "Say, '*no sé.*'"

"*No sé.*" She muttered the phrase under her breath. "*No sé.* What does it mean?"

"I don't know."

She rolled her eyes. "I'll sound like an idiot."

He stared into her until she fidgeted under his gaze.

"Fine." She checked the hat to make sure her hair was tucked tight to give her as androgynous an appearance as possible then smudged her face with dirt. She wasn't fair-skinned and might be able to pass for Latina, but there was no point in taking chances. "Ready," she said.

"Just stay close."

"*Sí, ese,*" she said, imitating Sebastian.

Xavier's mouth curled up a notch at the corners, and she smiled in return. Damn, it felt good to see him look at her like that. As if she hadn't betrayed him. As if he cared for her.

His eyes darkened. His smile died.

Moment over.

"Let's go." He moved forward, one hand on the butt of his gun.

Keeping her gaze on the ground, she matched her step with Xavier's, wondering what his sister would do when they confronted her. They were close once, but would that bond hold? Or would she turn them in?

Bethany's grip on the weapon at her side tightened. Heads down, they hurried down the middle of the camp, reaching the far end just in time to see the game breaking up and people dispersing. The players laughed, slapping each other and from their tone, bragging.

The clank of a bell sounded through the evening air. Bethany jumped. What was that about? She looked up at Xavier.

"I think it was the dinner bell. Move it."

With the crowd ahead of them, they dogged Eva as she headed toward one of the many scrap-wood shacks that made up the border of the camp.

"Follow me," Xavier whispered.

Bethany hurried after him, her heart racing. The sound of arguing caught her attention. She looked over her shoulder—hostages came in from the fields under escort, haggard and filthy beneath the rags they used as clothes—and she ran into a soldier.

The FARC soldier wasn't tall, but he was solid. His black hair clipped short and his skin tanned. He wore a green flight jacket with "Smith" embroidered on the pocket and an American flag on the other side.

She felt the blood drain from her face. She and Xavier were dead. She was sure of it. And it was her fault.

Smith glared at her. For a moment, there was no sound but that of her blood pumping in her ears.

He snapped a phrase at her.

She stared. Frozen.

"Ella lo siente," Xavier said, and then he grabbed her hand, pulling her around him and in Eva's direction. *"Prisa"*

The soldier put a hand on her shoulder, stopping her, and asked her something in Spanish.

"No sé," Bethany whispered.

Smith's brows shot up.

Bethany kept her lips pressed together to keep from babbling and she looked at Xavier.

Without hesitation he pushed himself between her and Smith and started talking. Smith glared, but Xavier stared him down, speaking fast. Despite Xavier's explaining, the doubt in Smith's eyes didn't fade. He wasn't buying what story Xavier was spinning.

Bethany looked around, searching for an escape. They might be able to run for it. Most of the people were headed toward the dining tent and the soldiers with the hostages seemed preoccupied.

Xavier said something else, and Smith grabbed Bethany's

arm, getting her attention. In those seconds of assessing the area, the soldier's expression transformed from suspicion to something new.

She looked to Xavier. Follow my lead, he mouthed.

Trusting him, she nodded.

With her in tow and Xavier following, Smith pulled her into one of the huts, and Bethany realized what it was Smith wanted.

Her.

Hell no.

There was no time to think, to accuse or to wonder what Xavier planned when every part of her brain and body screamed for her to run.

She jerked her arm out of Smith's grasp, but he grabbed her shirt and pulled her back. In seconds, he shoved her up against the wall and pinned her arms over her head, grinning and talking to her in Spanish.

Bethany bit her lip and closed her eyes.

I trust you, Xavier.

Seconds later, she was free. She opened her eyes. Xavier and Smith were on the ground, grappling. She watched the fight and it looked odd. Slow. Nothing like a Hollywood movie.

But she felt like a Hollywood heroine as she stood, watching and wringing her hands.

A quick glance around the room told her there was nothing to help her. Nothing big enough to use as a weapon.

The men broke apart. Bethany kicked Smith in the head.

He shook it off, but in those few seconds, Xavier was on his back, his arm around Smith's neck in a choke hold. Fifteen seconds later, the soldier passed out.

"Xavier?" Bethany dropped to her knees beside him. "Are you okay?"

His arm still around Smith's neck, he glanced at her, and she saw something unexpected in his eyes. Fear. "Look away," he said. "Now."

Sitting up, he adjusted his hands around Smith's neck.

She knew what he was going to do. What he had to do.

Bethany swallowed the bile that rose to her throat and did as Xavier asked.

Minutes later, Xavier pulled her to him, his arms around her, his head pressed against hers.

"I am so sorry," he whispered.

"It's not your fault," Bethany said, covering his arms with hers and holding on tight. There was no fault. No blame. They both did what had to be done.

"It wasn't my first choice," Xavier stressed, his voice thick. "He wasn't buying the story and the options were limited."

She nodded. "It's okay."

"It's not," Xavier argued. He pulled her closer. Squeezing her. "You should know that despite what's happened between us, I would *never* put you in true danger. I would never let anyone hurt you."

She did. He wasn't that kind of guy. "I know."

Still, his words echoed through her. Never put her in danger. Never let anyone hurt her. The vehemence behind the simple statement sounded like the Xavier before her betrayal. The way he held her felt almost like absolution.

Time stilled and dragged as she waiting, praying that now he'd come back to her. Want her.

Forgive her.

Instead, he released her. "We should hurry. I want to catch Eva before she goes to dinner, and this body won't remain hidden forever."

Bethany rubbed her arms as the heat in his eyes died, and she knew that regret and his apology were the only things he was going to offer.

It wasn't enough. Not by far. She wanted more.

She wanted Xavier.

* * *

Once, he thought he understood women. A little. Xavier caught the pained looked on Bethany's face and realized he didn't know a damn thing.

She was still upset, but it didn't seem to be about Smith. Though it should be. God knew, he was still shaken. Choking someone to death was as personal as killing got.

He scrubbed his face with his hand as they, once again, headed toward Eva's hut.

Seeing that soldier on Bethany, trying to hurt her…

He'd seen red. Hot, bright red that wiped out everything but the object of the rage. Only years of training and experience had kept him from screaming at Smith to get off his woman.

He'd never enjoyed killing someone before. It was always part of the job. This time, he'd felt actual pleasure at the deed until he'd seen Bethany's face.

Her wide eyes. Her fear. Her horror when she realized what he was going to do.

That had shaken him as much as seeing her in danger. And while he had to do what was needed, he didn't want her to watch. If she had, neither would ever come back from it.

She wasn't his anymore, but still…

Next, he'd be reading romance novels and drinking Chardonnay. He reclaimed his focus. He had bigger worries than Bethany's emotional well-being. He had Eva.

Had she really joined the enemy?

Xavier dreaded the answer he sensed was coming but didn't let it slow him. Instead, he increased his pace and in less than a minute, reached Eva's hut. Xavier didn't break stride but opened the door and went in.

Eva sat on a cot, an M16 next to her. Her eyes widened at the intrusion, and in seconds, the M16 was in her hand and pointing at them.

Xavier stopped. Hands out where Eva could see them.

Eva looked the same. Long, smooth hair, warm brown eyes with an underlay of "don't mess with me," and the tattoo for Miguel on her wrist. Even the M16 in her hand fit the image of his memory since she'd fought at his side when they were both member's of RADEC.

But the fact she held a weapon pointed at *him* was new and disturbing.

"Hello, little sister." His attention on the M16, hoping she'd put it down and prove him an idiot for ever thinking that she would betray him and their people.

"What are you doing here, Xavier?" Eva asked, her gaze fixed on him. She didn't lower the weapon. Not an inch. Not an iota.

He shook his head. What had they done to her?

For a heartbeat, Xavier didn't know how to respond. There were no answers and a hundred questions circling through his head, all vying for attention and demanding an answer.

"Why are you here?" Eva pushed.

She wasn't FARC, he told himself. They'd brainwashed her. It wouldn't be the first time that a prisoner became a captor. When people were left with nothing, they made a family from the nearest group of people.

Even when the people were the enemy.

"I've come to take you home," he replied, glad for once that Bethany couldn't speak Spanish. It would make it easier to break her FARC indoctrination if he didn't have to watch what he said.

He took a step toward Eva. Her trigger finger didn't tighten. A good sign. "Is that how you greet your brother?" he reminded, nodding at the weapon. "Is that how you greet family?"

Eva flinched at the last word, and the gun in her hand wavered. He held his breath.

Then her arm steadied.

He stilled, trying not to show his disappointment.

"No, but it's how I greet her." Eva shifted the muzzle, pointing it at Bethany, her voice low and dangerous. "Now answer me. What do you want?"

Xavier stared at her. He'd hoped this would be easier. That his presence would be enough.

He'd hoped wrong.

"What is going on?" Bethany interrupted. Her eyes were glued to the M16.

"We're talking," Xavier said, switching to English. "Just stay calm."

Eva laughed, but it was harder, harsher, than he remembered. "Where did you get the girl?" she prodded.

"She is a friend."

"A girlfriend?" Eva guessed, one eyebrow arched.

"Was."

"Was? Who screwed up? You or her?"

For a flicker, Eva was the sister he remembered. The one that teased him about his dating habits.

Perhaps she wasn't as far gone as he thought.

He glanced at Bethany. He could say that Bethany betrayed him but he suspected that Eva would take the news poorly. "Doesn't matter."

"Of course it does. You came all this way." Her eyes narrowed. "It was her, wasn't it?"

Yep, she was pissed. He'd called that right though it was a small comfort. "Let it go, Eva," Xavier said.

"Wow, she must have done something beyond stupid."

Even when they were acting nuts, little sisters were a pain. "I said, let it go."

Eva hesitated and he could almost see the wheels spinning in her head. Finally, she shrugged. "How did you find me?"

He nodded toward Bethany. "Her sister. She told us you were here."

"She is FARC?"

Xavier sighed. This conversation was already taking more time than he wanted. The other soldiers might discover the dead soldier at any moment. Once that happened, they'd start searching huts.

They needed to move past the unimportant details and get down to what mattered.

"I know that being held hostage can be confusing," he suggested, keeping his voice low and ignoring her last question. "It's easy to sympathize with your captors. To come to see them as your family."

Eva rolled her eyes. "It's nothing like that."

"Then what are you doing here?" he asked reining in his growing irritation. People with Stockholm syndrome believed in what they said. He'd have to push harder. Challenge her.

"Helping out," she answered, flashing him a defiant look that he knew all too well.

"Helping FARC?"

Her dark brown eyes bored into his. "I take it you do not approve?"

He stared back, wanting to scream, shout and shake sense into her. He controlled the urge. She was too old for bullying by her brother, and it wouldn't help break FARC's hold on her. In fact, it might make her dig in her heels.

Truth seemed to be the easiest way to go. "They killed our brother. They broke up our family," he countered. "Of course I don't approve, and neither would the Eva I remember."

Eva stiffened. "This war killed our brother, and I plan to end it. That is why I am here. That is why I am helping FARC. And that is all you need to know."

"They brainwashed you," Xavier stated, clenching his fists at his side. Why did she have to fight so hard? Be so stubborn?

She shook her head. "They didn't do this to me, Xavier. I'm not one of those weak people who succumb to their story because I have nothing else to hold on to."

Xavier's gut tightened.

"I was FARC long before you walked through that door." Eva looked at him, sympathy in her dark brown eyes. "The kidnapping? The message for the money? The threats against my life?" She left the questions open, hanging and waiting for Xavier to piece it all together.

"Your idea," he whispered as grief overwhelmed him. It was like losing Miguel all over again and for a moment, he forgot to breathe.

"Yes," she said. "But I did it to save you, too, you moron. You are still my family. Still my brother. They were going to kill you. I lost Miguel. I didn't want to lose you, as well."

His little sister was a terrorist. Xavier paced to the other side of the hut. "I don't believe it."

"You should," Eva persisted, her voice strong. Sure.

It was almost impossible to understand, to comprehend. He couldn't deny that Bethany had hurt him with her betrayal. Wounded him so deeply that he felt as if he could lift his shirt and see blood pouring from his chest.

But this…this broke his heart. "I can't believe that Samantha was right. I can't."

He felt a hand on his shoulder. When he turned, it was Bethany. Her eyes were bright with tears. She might not understand the language, but she knew what had happened. He covered her hand with his.

"I am so sorry," she whispered.

"It's okay," he replied, though he wasn't sure anything would ever be okay again.

"Samantha?" Eva interrupted. "As in Samantha Darrow?"

The hairs on the back of Xavier's neck sprung upward, and he shunted the pain aside, bringing himself back to the situation at hand. If he wanted to mourn the loss of his sister, it would have to be later.

A FARC encampment wasn't the place to lose his shit.

Eva looked over at Bethany, growing recognition in her eyes. "What is your girlfriend's name?" she asked Xavier.

Taking a deep breath, Xavier swallowed the grief and pushed it down to a place where it couldn't touch him. He stepped in front of Bethany, putting himself between the two women. He locked his gaze on Eva.

Eva smiling. Fighting by his side. Standing at Miguel's grave, her hand in his.

He shook the images away.

The woman with the M16 was not Eva. She was a FARC solider. Nothing more.

Not his sister.

And he knew what FARC did—they took what didn't belong to them. They didn't deserve any explanations. "It doesn't matter who she is. We're leaving. You owe me that. Have fun with your war."

"Bethany?" Eva asked. "Bethany Darrow?"

"What?" Bethany replied.

Dammit.

He clenched his jaw tight. Bethany couldn't have known to keep silent. In the future, he was going to have to teach her more tricks of the trade—and some Spanish.

In the future? He shook his head. That was a thought better left for later.

Eva continued, switching to English. "Since you are my brother, I'll give you the option of leaving. But not her." She nodded toward Bethany. "She is taking her sister's place."

"Like hell I am," Bethany contradicted.

"Did I offer you a choice?" Eva cocked the weapon.

"She leaves with me," Xavier said.

"Why? She is nothing to you. You said so."

"Oh," Bethany uttered.

He glanced back at Bethany. Her face was pale with a green tint. He'd seen that shade before—on the face of a man who was gut-punched. "You never know when to shut up, Eva. You never do," Xavier said, forcing his voice level and low when all he wanted to do was yell. "And you don't know everything."

"Well, neither do you. She stays as a replacement for her sister."

Xavier clenched and unclenched his hands. This was degenerating into a battle of wills, and with Eva, those were almost impossible to win. She was as stubborn as a burro. "Bethany, walk out."

"Not without you."

Great. Two stubborn women. "Go. I'll be right behind you."

"You never listen to me," Eva rambled, huffing in exasperation. "Don't worry, I won't kill her. She is too valuable. But I can hurt her if you try to take her."

She wasn't kidding. Eva would do what was needed to accomplish what she wanted. Even as a child, she was fearless and driven. As his sister, he loved that about her. Nurtured it.

As his enemy, it was a pain in his ass. "I'll stay instead," he said in Spanish.

"There's no one to pay for you. They'll just kill you." Eva stiffened. "I need her. Not you."

Not even the dark place in his gut could contain that verbal punch. Xavier ground his teeth, trying to make her last words change.

And the sound of shouting penetrated the walls of the thin shack.

Someone had found the body. Crap.

Eva frowned at Xavier. "I don't know what you did, but you need to leave. I can't protect you if they find you here. Go."

She turned her gaze to Bethany. "You stay."

Bethany paled, but she pulled her shoulders down and stepped out of his shadow. "No."

* * *

Eva looked ready to shoot, and Bethany steeled herself.

She thought of her mother. Her sister. They'd been apart too long, and Eva wasn't going to stop their family reunion.

She took a step back toward the door. Eva matched her, taking a step forward. Once again, Xavier placed himself between her and danger.

Bethany touched the small of his back. "It's okay," she reassured. "I can handle this."

"Listen to her, brother," Eva said.

Bethany hesitated, not missing the anxiety in Eva's voice. The FARC soldier was pushed into a place she didn't want to be—forced to choose between her cause and her brother. Bethany suspected that if forced, she'd pick her brother.

Xavier might not think so. He was too withdrawn to see anything right now, but she heard the quiver beneath Eva's bravado and she didn't miss the way Eva looked at Xavier, a combination of hero-worship and admiration.

"I am," Xavier said. "She's nuts. And we're leaving."

"I am not nuts," Bethany protested. "But you're right. I'm walking out with you." The shouting grew closer. It wouldn't be long now.

"How do you plan to leave, *chica?*" Eva asked. "I am the one with the loaded gun."

"Through the door, and you won't stop us because you won't hurt your brother," Bethany said, calling her bluff.

Eva leveled the gun at her chest, hesitated and then lowered it to her leg. "I will not kill you. You are money to us. But I can make it so you can't run."

"Good luck with that," Bethany said, sounding more flippant that she felt. "Let's go, Xavier."

"About time," Xavier said. He opened the door for Bethany.

The gunshot echoed in the small hut and kicked up the dirt next to Bethany's foot, making her jump and leaving her ears ringing.

"Don't think I won't do it," Eva dared.

The shouting grew closer. Too close. They'd be here in minutes. Seconds. Bethany's heart pounded. She glanced at the two brackets on either side of the door and the rough two-by-four next to it. Hands shaking, she slid the wood into the brackets. A crude lock, but it might buy them a few seconds.

"Dammit, Xavier," Eva cursed. "You couldn't just leave, could you?"

Xavier stalked over to his sister in response. "I should have done this five minutes ago." He grabbed the barrel of the weapon.

"Oh, crap," Bethany whispered.

Eva glared at him, and for a moment, Bethany wondered if she'd called it wrong. That Eva would choose FARC over Xavier.

Eva's cheeks bloomed pink, and she relaxed her grip, her knuckles going from white to tan. Xavier yanked the weapon from her hands. "One day, you are going to come to your senses and when you do, you are going to beg my forgiveness."

"I might say the same." She sank down onto the cot.

He shook his head. "Never." He handed the gun to Bethany. "Hold this. Eva isn't allowed to play with weapons anymore."

There was a pounding on the door. Bethany caught Eva's name, but that was it. "Now what?" she asked.

"That way," Xavier said, heading to the back wall. "Just be ready to run. As long as we stay ahead of them, they won't be able to get a shot. Just don't stop moving. Don't lose me."

"And if I do?"

"Don't." He raised his foot and kicked out the board in one thrust. Squeezing through, he held out his hand.

Behind her, the door splintered. She slid between the planks, took Xavier's hand and ran.

Chapter 14

"What now," Bethany asked, squinting into the dark ahead of them. The sky had been purple when they entered the compound. Now, with the help of the canopy, it wasn't black, but it was close, and trees were turning into mere shadows.

Crashing and gunfire followed them, making her cringe.

"Keep moving," Xavier said, helping her over a broken branch.

"I don't think they're going to give up." She tripped and caught herself before she fell. Unlike the Colombian army, FARC would not be dissuaded from pursuit in the dark. She meant money, Xavier meant revenge and there were few stronger motivations.

She'd survive being captured, but if they caught Xavier…she shuddered at the thought. There was little doubt that they'd make an example of him. It wouldn't be the first time they'd used scare tactics to remind the government of who ruled the jungle.

She grabbed Xavier's arm, slowing him. "We need to lose them. Backtrack and wait for them to pass us."

"Backtrack?" His face remained impassive, but the doubt in his voice told her what he thought of the idea.

"I know it seems simplistic," Bethany pressed, "but we can't run forever."

She grazed a tree and sent birds squawking into the night.

Xavier groaned and she knew what he was thinking—that she might as well have sent up a flare that said, "Here I am." But he didn't stop and didn't agree.

"Please," she begged, not caring how it sounded. "I'm not a pro, but if people wander away on trips, I am skilled enough to find them. I can make this work. *We* can make this work."

Sweat beaded Bethany's forehead, and the dampness had nothing to do with the heat. FARC still lagged behind, but it wouldn't take long for them to catch up. Not with flashlights and determination driving them.

"Okay, let's do this," Xavier conceded. "And fast."

She almost cried in relief. It wasn't much of a chance, but it was better than nothing. Using the hem of her T-shirt, she wiped her brow. "Stay in your tracks." Bethany indicated, though in looking down, even with her eyes adjusted to the darkness her tracks were almost nonexistent. "Break some branches."

Two minutes later they'd retraced their path, making it as obvious as possible that they'd gone on. Behind them, birds took flight, squawking. FARC was close now. "Time to hide," Xavier confirmed.

She nodded, adrenaline making her shake. Being careful to leave no trace, they wormed their way off the path, hunkered down and waited.

Despite the increasing darkness, the air remained heated and thick. The scent of moss and decay filled her nose. Would she ever get the smell out of her head?

Beams of light came into view as the FARC soldiers followed the trail they'd created.

"Think they'll fall for it?" Bethany asked. They were thirty feet from the trail, and while the dense foliage was more than enough cover, she still felt exposed.

"It's your idea. What do you think?"

Their lives were hanging on her idea. The responsibility unnerved her. She glanced at Xavier, a mere shape beside her.

He does this all the time, she realized. The sudden comprehension made her blink in surprise. Every time he went out, he took that responsibility. Sure, his men were skilled. Trained to fight. To kill. To do what was needed to accomplish the mission.

But he was the leader, and it was up to him to make sure they all came home alive. Even her. The unexpected insight boggled her mind. "How do you do it?" she whispered.

"Do what?"

"This? Save people. Take that responsibility."

"I never thought about it," he revealed. "Now be quiet."

The explanation didn't quiet her awe.

Seconds later, a beam from a flashlight swung over. She held her breath, even though her head told her there was no way they could hear her breathing. The beam kept going, creating an arc of light through the jungle. She found herself straining to hear the soldiers but caught only a few quasi-familiar words. *Prisa. Esta manera.*

Then a familiar, feminine voice captured her attention. *Eva.*

Xavier's breath caught at hearing his sister, and though the sound was almost imperceptible, it broke Bethany's heart to hear it. She slid her hand over to Xavier's, touching his fingertips with hers. He didn't pull away, but neither did he take her hand.

A tense minute later, the lights went past them and continued north, following their trail. "I'm sorry," she whispered as they waited for them to disappear out of sight.

"For what?" Xavier said.

"Eva."

Xavier pulled his hand from hers. Rising to his knees, he gazed down the path. "It's clear. Let's go."

So, he didn't want to discuss his sister. She couldn't blame him. He was a leader and focused on escape. She wished she could compartmentalize like that. If Samantha had turned traitor, she'd be talking to everyone, working it out with words.

But Xavier wasn't her.

She took a deep breath. Talking could wait. "What next? I can guide, but escaping the enemy is your forte, not mine."

"We go back the way we came and get our packs, providing they haven't found them," Xavier explained.

"After that?" Bethany asked.

Xavier headed toward the trail. "More walk. Less talk."

She hoped he had a plan. The jungle remained silent around them, the birds and insects having scattered or gone quiet at the commotion of the humans, and the *less talk* part of Xavier's command was killing her.

She needed to know what was going on. Not knowing was worse. And if he wouldn't talk about Eva then he needed to give her something to focus on besides a hazy future. "Are we going to get out of this?"

"Yes."

He sounded so sure. "How?" she pressed.

"Tonight."

"That's a *when*. Not a *how*." They both knew that traipsing through the jungle was dangerous. "Isn't the jungle at night a death wish?"

"By morning, there will be men everywhere and they will be expecting us. That decreases the odds." He hesitated. "Plus, that'll give them time to set traps to try and capture us."

"Traps?" The word brought up imagines of frond-covered pits.

"Guerrilla warfare," Xavier stated. "Snares that can run a

stake through your legs. Trip wires. Traps designed to maim. Not kill."

Bethany chilled despite the heated jungle air. "I can handle that," she affirmed, not sure who she was trying to convince. "I can be careful."

Xavier stopped in the path, his face just visible in the remaining light. "Don't make the mistake of thinking they aren't skilled. Some are no more than farmers who can't hit the side of a building, but many are trained. Always go with the assumption that they are as good as we are. Maybe better, since this is their turf. We leave tonight." He began walking again.

Bethany sighed. She knew why he was forcing this—he wouldn't be the one to blunder into a trap. It would be her. Visions of herself with a sharp stick in her leg raced across her mind, followed by visions of herself as a FARC hostage. And then Xavier captured because he wouldn't abandon her.

He was suggesting this because of her. *For her.*

Just when she thought she couldn't stand another layer of guilt.

Guilty conscience or not, she needed to show him that she was trustworthy despite her sketchy track record. "Let's start walking," she suggested, keeping her voice steady. "Maybe we can find a place to set another zip-line in the morning." Though the thought of speeding across *herida roja* again made her nauseous.

"Walk?" Xavier declined. "There's no way we'll keep ahead of them. Not now. We're going to steal a jeep."

They'd dodged two more tracking parties to recover the packs, rifle, ammo and find a suitable locale to watch the FARC encampment. Lit with a combination of oil and battery-powered halogen lanterns, there was enough light to illuminate both the compound and the surrounding jungle. It seemed that most of the soldiers were gone—searching for her and Xavier, no doubt. She lowered her binoculars.

Still, there were enough men milling about to make her nervous.

"No one will expect us to steal a jeep," Xavier insisted, his voice firm and strong enough to almost make her believe it.

"It is a little ballsy," she confirmed. "But also insane."

"That's the beauty." Xavier chuckled, a surprising sound considering the last hour's ordeal. "We move fast. Keep our eyes peeled. Stay frosty."

"Frosty?" she huffed, wiping the sweat off her forehead.

He raised a brow. "You know what I mean."

She smiled. "I do. So, how does one steal a guarded jeep?"

"Hot-wire."

It figured. "How do we keep them from following? Shoot the tires?"

"No," Xavier replied. "We'll need to permanently disable them. A few good explosions should do the trick."

Bethany frowned. "With what? Sebastian has the dynamite."

"Doesn't matter. Dynamite is too iffy," Xavier explained. "Too long a fuse and FARC can toss the stick before it explodes. Too short and we'll get caught in the blast."

She remembered the blast from the bridge, the men plunging to their death, the few who were caught in the middle of the blast, and her stomach rolled over.

"We need C4 and a detonator," Xavier said. "Which means we need to hit their weapons cache."

Bethany hesitated. "Do we know if they even have one?"

"They do."

"It seems reckless." There were too many variables. Too many ways for one or both of them to get shot or captured.

"Perhaps but anything less is fixable. Do you want to get away only to have them capture us five miles down the road?"

"I vote no on that scenario," Bethany replied.

"My thoughts, as well." He shook his head. "I wished to hell we'd grabbed a few C4 bricks while we were rescuing Samantha."

She shrugged. "You were busy trying to save us."

He didn't reply, and she knew what he was thinking. That it wasn't saving Samantha that had muddled his thoughts. It was her betrayal and Samantha's revelations.

"Do you think they'll have C4?" Bethany asked when the silence stretched her nerves almost to the point of breaking.

"I sure as hell hope so," he revealed. He looked at her, his eyes dark and worried. "Or we are screwed."

Bethany nodded. "Okay. Tell me what you want me to do."

Xavier smoothed back his hair. "How good a shot are you?"

"Good enough to keep you alive."

He sat up, searched the pack and handed her an earpiece. "Here. I'll need you to be my eyes."

Next, he handed her his rifle and a box of bullets. "Use this. It'll be easier to sight than a handgun."

Her hands shaking, Bethany took the weapon. She was committed now. Hell, she'd been committed the moment she stepped off the plane. She knew it. Xavier knew it.

"Do not fire unless there is no choice," Xavier instructed. "I'd rather them not know we're here until we have the jeep in Drive."

Bethany fitted the earpiece over her ear and gave a sharp nod. "I'll guide you."

Xavier fitted his earpiece in as well and picked up the night-vision binoculars. "Be careful. When I tell you, head for the jeep."

"Whatever you say." His life was in her hands. The thought made her shiver. What if she failed? What if he were killed? "Xavier?"

He froze. "Having seconds thoughts?"

Yes. "No," she replied, shaking her head. What if she let him down, again?

He tilted her chin up, his mouth inches from hers. She closed her eyes, and for a heartbeat, he was the Xavier from before. The man who made love to her. The man who saved her sister.

Her protector.

He caressed her cheek with his thumb. "I trust you to keep me safe," he whispered. His breath warm against her mouth, and it brought tears to her eyes.

Then he was gone, fading into the foliage.

"Do you hear me?" His voice crackled over the earpiece, all business and no tenderness.

Back to work. "Loud and clear," she replied. Hunkering down, she sighted the camp through the rifle scope.

"Heading down. I'm going to go around the right side and enter from there. I'll be heading for the third building. The one covered in netting."

The locale was fifty yards away. Not too hard a shot but not easy either under these conditions. "I have your back," she said.

Five minutes later, she spied a dark figure step out from the jungle behind one of the buildings. He raised a hand and gave a short wave.

"Hi to you, too," Bethany greeted.

"How's it looking?" Xavier asked.

She sighted the area between him and the bunker. Someone was making rounds. "Stay put. We have a player near the bunker."

"Stationary or moving?"

"Moving. I'll tell you when."

The sentry hesitated, lit a cigarette and continued his rounds. "Go now," Bethany said.

Pressed against the side of the building, Xavier edged toward the weapons.

Bethany scanned the area again. How did snipers do this? Stay focused and immobile while adrenaline saturated every fiber of their body. Movement caught her eye. "We have a new player," Bethany informed. "He's at your two. In front of the building to your right."

"What's he doing?" Xavier whispered.

She squinted into the dark. "Either he's short or sitting in a chair," she remarked. "There's a barrel in the way. I can only see him from the shoulders up."

"Probably guarding hostages while the others are looking for us," Xavier guessed, "Anyone else close?"

"No." She wondered how much longer that bit of luck would last.

She watched while Xavier moved behind the guard's building then disappeared down the far side. "What are you doing?" she whispered. "Xavier?"

He didn't respond. Seconds later, the guard disappeared.

"Xavier?" she whispered his name again. Still no answer.

Her heart pounded hard enough to make her press her hand against her sternum. "Dammit, answer me. Are you okay?"

Five more beats went past. "Keep your panties on," Xavier demanded, his voice breathing life back into her.

"Please don't do that again," she said, almost sobbing in relief.

"I'll try. Now, can you keep it together? We're almost done."

She took a deep breath. He was right. It was time to stay frosty. "I'm good." She wiped her eyes surprised to find them wet. "And you're good to move."

She watched while Xavier went across the ten feet of dirt and slipped into the netted bunker.

"Is it the cache?" she asked.

"The netted bunker is always the cache," Xavier said. "We have C4."

"Best news today," Bethany concluded with a grin.

"I'm going back the way I came. Maintain silence unless there's a problem. Meet me at the vehicles in twenty." She watched as he slipped out from under the netting then sighed in relief when he entered the jungle without incident.

"I'll hurry. See you in ten," she countered, her heart beating with hope for the first time since Xavier discovered her secret.

Twenty minutes later, she must have inhaled too much moss to think she could skirt the camp in that amount of time in the dark while watching for the occasional booby trap.

"Where are you?" Xavier's voice came over the headset, startling her, and confirming her tardiness.

"On my way," she replied, keeping her voice low. "It's taking longer than I thought." The light coming from the camp helped, but it also created shadows that caused the occasional misstep.

"Get the lead out. I have the jeeps wired and ready to go."

"Wired?"

"The C4 is wired to the headlights."

She shuddered at the imagery. "That's gruesome."

"Necessary."

"No argument from me," she replied, taking a short step as she twisted her ankle. She stopped and flexed it. No harm, but the last thing they needed was another problem. "I'll be there in three. Now let me concentrate."

"I'll be waiting."

She clicked the earpiece off in time to hear something rustle the bushes. The hairs on the back of Bethany's neck rose. She squinted into the shadows. Was something there? FARC was her first thought, but she dismissed it. They wouldn't watch her. Not even for a few seconds. They'd take her at gunpoint.

Attention focused on the jungle, Bethany counted to ten. The leaves remained still and silent. She managed a grim smile at her own active imagination.

She turned to continue, and out of the corner of her eye, she caught movement. Once again, the hairs on her neck prickled alarm. Dammit, there *was* something there. Another jaguar? There wasn't much else. Besides puma, they were the only large predators in the jungle.

"Don't I ever get a break," she muttered. She tapped her earpiece. "Xavier, I think we have a problem. One that requires catnip."

"You are kidding me," Xavier said. She winced at the anger in his voice. "Back away. Slowly. I'm already on my way."

She took a step back. The predator followed her. "Hurry," she whispered.

Another step. Still, it tracked her. She stopped. It stopped.

Clever beast. She swallowed the fear rising in her gut. But not that clever. Not like her. Bethany slung the rifle over her shoulder. She didn't want to shoot the cat but given no other option, she would do what was needed and they'd deal with escape as it came.

There would be no escape if she were dead. Keeping her gaze on the shadow, she slid her hand towards her handgun and unsnapped the leather strap that held it in place.

"Don't bother," the shadow said, the command followed by the click of a gun being cocked.

Bethany froze. She knew that voice. The shadow moved forward. "And as long as we're talking, put your hands where I can see them."

Bethany raised her hands. "Hello, Eva."

Xavier's sister smiled at her. "Did you think you could get away?"

Bethany shrugged. "Did you think we wouldn't try?"

Eva sighed. "That's why I came back and left everyone else to beat the bushes. I know my brother. *Testarudo.*"

Bethany didn't know what she said, but she could guess its meaning.

Eva continued, "Call my brother. Tell him that the jaguar ran away and that you will be there in a few minutes."

Bethany remembered all she'd read about kidnappings. The books said that the victim should cooperate. Don't fight. Don't be stubborn. And don't question.

But the thought of cooperating with Eva made her nauseous. Bethany crossed her arms over her chest. "No. I'm not helping you."

Eva's eyes widened. "Are you crazy? Do it. He will be here soon."

"So? I can see you shooting me, but you won't hurt Xavier." Bethany's mouth twisted into a knowing smile. "You love your brother. You wouldn't hurt a hair on his head."

Eva stiffened, and Bethany knew she'd drawn first metaphorical blood. Breathing hard, Eva hesitated then stepped forward, pressing the gun against Bethany's sternum. "Why fight me? I have the gun."

Why indeed? There was no great answer to being stubborn other than she was pissed. Sure, she'd lied to Xavier but Eva had almost destroyed him.

Bitch.

"Maybe because I know you won't pull the trigger," Bethany said. Snapping her hand downward, she grabbed the barrel of the weapon, pushing it down and sideways, and swinging her other hand towards the woman's jaw.

Eva didn't let go but yanked the weapon back. Bethany's fist swished through the air. Missed. She tightened her grip on the weapon, pulling harder.

Then her jaw exploded in pain, and she dropped to her knees. She had missed. Eva hadn't.

"Do not try that again," Eva warned. Yanking the rifle from Bethany's shoulder, she tossed it aside and did the same with her handgun.

Bethany looked up. Eva clenched and unclenched her fingers, wincing. "Good, I hope it's broken," Bethany said, rubbing her jaw.

Eva jerked Bethany to her feet then stepped back, leveling the weapon at Bethany's chest. "Are you ready to do as I ask?"

Bethany shook her head. "No. You take me and he'll come

after me. That's the kind of man he is. Haven't you done enough to him already?"

Eva frowned and her dark eyes narrowed. "What I did? How about you? I may not know the details, but I suspect he might be grateful to leave you behind."

Bethany sucked air between her teeth and clenched her hands into tight fists as she fought the urge to launch herself at Eva. "What I did was stupid. Stupid and weak and I would do anything to take it back. *Anything.*" Her eyes watered with angry tears. "But I can't, so I have to live with the knowledge that I hurt someone I care for.

"But it is nothing compared to your betrayal," she retorted, her voice rising. "Did you see your brother's face? Did you see?"

Eva took another step back. "Shut up."

She wouldn't shut up. Couldn't stop talking now that she'd started. "You can tell yourself what you want, whatever lets you sleep, but we both know who the real villain is."

"I did not—"

"You betrayed him, Eva." Bethany almost spat the words, anger at Eva's selfishness taking over. "You turned your back on Xavier and everything he fought for and now you want to do it again."

"I had no choice," Eva declared, her voice sharp.

She meant it, Bethany realized. The power and anger in Eva's words were as tangible as the weapon in her hand. But there was more. There was regret. And maybe she could use it to turn Eva. Give Xavier back his sister.

If she brought Eva back to him, he might forgive her as well. "There is always a choice."

"Not in Colombia," Eva argued.

"Even in Colombia," Bethany countered. "Don't screw up your relationship with your brother. Help us escape. Come with us. He'll forgive you."

"No, he won't," Eva declared.

Bethany took a step forward. "He will. He loves you. You should have heard him talk about you and Miguel. How you grew up on the streets. How you always took care of each other. How you lost your brother."

"He spoke of Miguel?" Eva asked, surprised.

"Yes. It broke his heart to lose him. Don't do this, Eva. Don't make him lose you, too. Come home."

"He hasn't spoken of Miguel since his funeral." Eva touched her mouth, and for a split second was lost in the past. In a blink and a sigh, she was back in the present. "Call Xavier. If he comes here, I will have no choice but to take him, as well. Do you want that?"

"No." Bethany sighed. So much for trying to heal a rift. For fighting.

She tapped her earpiece. "Xavier, whatever it was ran away. I'll be there in a few minutes."

"No need," Xavier claimed. He stepped out from the bushes and pointed his gun at Eva. "I'm here."

Chapter 15

"How long have you been standing there?" Bethany asked, her attention bounced from the weapon in his hand, to Eva then back again.

"Long enough," Xavier answered. And longer than he cared to admit. He was faster and quieter than either Bethany or Eva, and he'd arrived in time to hear both Bethany's confession and her attempt to talk Eva into coming with them.

As much as he didn't want to admit it, the catch in her voice as she made her confession touched him. Made him want to pull her close. To dry her tears away and tell her everything would be okay.

He wanted to believe her claim of regret. Wanted it so much it made him ache, but doubt whispered in his ear, making him cautious.

Eva wasn't so swayed. The only way Eva changed her mind or direction was when Eva decided to do so. Otherwise, she didn't budge.

"Bethany, head toward the jeeps," Xavier said.

"Take a single step and I will kill you," Eva vowed, her weapon still pointed at Bethany's heart.

His sister had killed in the name of freedom. He'd seen her pull the trigger with little regret, but to shoot Bethany now would be murder in cold blood. Some things weren't lost no matter what changed or who you tried to be. He stared down Eva using his best big brother glare. "You forget that I know you. Bethany, go."

"Don't. I will shoot." Eva's voice broke. "I swear."

"Go," Xavier ordered. Bethany said she trusted him. Now was the time to prove it.

Bethany gave a curt nod and pushed her shoulders back, the epitome of a soldier. Proud. Strong. Fearless. She gave Eva a nonchalant shrug. "Good luck." Picking up the discarded weapons, Bethany walked away.

When she was out of sight, Eva growled in anger and holstered her weapon. "Thanks for nothing," she snarled, facing Xavier with her hands on her hips.

"Did you think I'd let you take her?"

Eva gave him a halfhearted shrug. "I'm your sister. You might. Besides, you're angry with her."

"Not that angry," Xavier corrected, surprised to find the words to be true. He hadn't forgiven Bethany. Not by far. But between the long walk to get to Bethany, the fear at seeing *Smith* try to assault her and her confession, the consuming rage faded to a dull roar. "Now, can I trust you to stay here or are you going to raise the alarm?"

Eva tossed her long hair with a careless hand. A familiar gesture courtesy of the girl he used to know. "Take her. Go."

He hesitated, hope urging him to extend the olive branch. "Come with me, *hermanita.* She was right. We're a family, and with family, there is forgiveness."

"You heard her little monologue?"

He nodded and held out his hand, willing her to take it. "Come home, Eva."

Instead, she took a step back, widening the space between them. Xavier let his arm drop.

Hands still on her hips, she glared at him with the arrogance of FARC. "I am doing you a courtesy to let you leave. Do not make this harder than it needs to be."

Who was this woman? He'd hoped...

Anger flickered back to life, and Xavier swallowed down his disappointment. "Don't come home, Eva. Ever."

"Your words were empty then?" Eva challenged. "There is forgiveness only when one does as you request? Only when someone does as Xavier thinks they should do?"

Xavier clenched his jaw. "No."

"That is what it sounds like," Eva persisted. "Forgiveness with strings attached. Really long strings."

He wanted to argue, but there was no arguing with FARC. And Eva was FARC now. He turned on his heel, heading back toward the jeeps.

"You tried," Bethany reiterated, stepping out of the shadows.

He didn't break pace.

"Maybe she'll come to her senses," Bethany offered.

Xavier clenched his jaw tight and reminded himself that she was trying to help. "I don't want to talk about this. We have a mission."

"You'll have to at some point," Bethany said.

Xavier stopped. "Do you think now is the time? Here?" He waved a hand toward the FARC encampment just in view to their right.

Bethany hesitated then continued toward the jeeps. "I guess not," she commented, the stiffness of the words belying her cool delivery.

Xavier rolled his eyes in exasperation. Sometimes, he wanted to shake some sense into her. She made him crazy with the way she twisted words. They passed a large mango tree—his marker—and all anger and tension faded as the mission took control.

Xavier touched Bethany's shoulder, bringing her to a halt. "We're here."

She shrugged his hand off, and he pushed the flash of irritation away.

"How does this work?" she asked, all business. "We have to drive the length of the camp."

"I know." It wasn't the best scenario, but there weren't any others. "We get in, gun it and hope for the best."

"Who drives?"

He grinned despite the tension. "I'm the man. Who do you think?"

Bethany didn't rise to the bait but shrugged and holstered her weapon. "I'll ride shotgun, as it were, and make sure we get out in one piece."

A chill washed over Xavier. Having her as sniper from the jungle was one thing, but this would be up close and personal and he didn't want her to step over that line. Not even for him. "I do not think that's a good idea."

"Why?" She raised a dark brow. "I'm not going to hide in the backseat while you take all the risk."

Laying low in the backseat was exactly what he wanted her to do. "You're not battle-tested, and this isn't your fight. It isn't your mission. It's mine. I'll take the risk. I just want to get you out in one piece."

Bethany looked up at nothing, blinking hard. Hell, was she going to cry? Then she looked back at him, her eyes dry. "I appreciate the sentiment, but this is my mission, too. It's my fault you found out about Eva."

"I needed to know," Xavier responded, though a part of him wished he'd remained ignorant.

"But not like this." Bethany flattened her hand against his

chest, as if sensing his heartache at losing Eva. Any remaining irritation fled at her touch. "Not hearing it from a stranger."

She looked up at him. "Don't take this away from me, Xavier. You need backup or we're both dead."

He shook his head.

Bethany continued, "You trusted me to guard your back when you went for the C4. Trust me again. I've earned it. Please. *Trust me.*"

Trust her? She wasn't talking about the escape. She was talking about what they had before he found out her lies.

And he wanted to trust her again. A little. He placed his hand over hers. Her skin was damp but smooth, and she was impossible to deny, despite everything she'd done. "Try not to kill anyone unless you have to."

She smiled up at him. All Bethany.

All his.

Just one kiss, he told himself. For luck. To make her feel better. He brought her hand to his mouth and kissed her palm.

Now who was lying, the sly voice in his head whispered.

Her eyes wide, she stared into his eyes, her silence saying more than words.

Fine, he was a liar. In this case, he could live with it. Xavier brought his mouth down on Bethany's, consumed by the need to feel her, to taste her, one more time.

Her breathing deepened, and she slid her hand up his chest, wrapping her arm around his neck and matching his passion with her own.

Mine. The primal urge overwhelmed him, intensified by adrenaline. Yanking her hat off, Xavier wound his fingers through Bethany's hair as he tasted the salt on her lips.

He kissed a path along her jaw then worked his way to her neck, wanting to forget the deceptions and pain. Wanting to go back to what they were.

Wanting Bethany.

A shout caught his attention, and Xavier pulled himself away, his heart pounding.

Bethany stared at him, her breathing harsh and hurried.

He looked toward the far end of the camp. The teams were returning. He took a deep breath. This was why he didn't like to bring women on a mission. Well, at least bring Bethany. She made him crazy. Made him forget who he was and where he was.

Still, it was up to him to save her. He took a deep breath and his pulse steadied. "Are you sure you want to do this?"

She grabbed her cap, held up her handgun, all business. "Let's go home."

The gorge was easier, Bethany decided as she crawled along the jungle floor towards the jeep, her head just a few inches away from Xavier's shoes. Less mess. A good view. And almost zero chance of someone shooting at her.

They reached the vehicle, and Xavier motioned for her to wait. She'd heard the expression "a minute felt like an eternity" but had never understood it until now.

The jeep rocked as Xavier crawled into the cab then stopped. Once again, time sputtered and struggled as they both waited to see if any of FARC noticed the movement.

Nothing but chatter punctuated with shouts drifted from the other end of the camp.

Xavier leaned over and motioned for her to get in. Bethany crawled inside and flattened herself on the bench seat, trying to keep below the jeep's profile.

Xavier lay on the floorboard, wires in hand. "Ready?" he whispered.

This wasn't like guiding Xavier through the encampment or shooting someone from a distance. Anyone she shot here would be close. She'd see their face. Watch them die.

They're terrorists, she reminded herself. They took your sister and they'll take you, if they don't kill you. They're the bad guys.

While the platitudes didn't quell the flock of butterflies in her stomach, neither did the butterflies quell her determination. Besides, maybe she'd get lucky and the soldiers wouldn't notice them until it was too late. "Ready."

"Remember to breathe," he said, touching the wires together. The jeep sputtered.

"Come on," Xavier said. He touched the wires again, and the engine came to life.

Someone shouted from the far end of the camp.

So much for not being noticed.

Bethany rose in the seat, sitting on her knees for better mobility. Xavier slid behind the wheel, shoved gears into place and pressed the pedal to the floor.

In seconds, they were speeding toward the road at the far end of the camp. Bethany counted five men running toward them, guns raised. Bile rose in her throat, and she swallowed it back.

"Hang on," Xavier shouted. She grabbed the dash as he jerked the jeep to one side and then another, zigzagging the vehicle and forcing the men to miss their shots.

But the camp wasn't that big, and in a few seconds they'd be on the soldiers and not even serpentining the jeep would keep them safe.

It was up to her.

She scanned the enemy. Ready. Watching. One of them focused on Xavier and raised his weapon.

Oh, hell no.

Breathe. Xavier's voice replaced the panic.

Bethany took a deep breath. Held it. And time slowed with her exhale, came to a halt and gave her time to notice the rage in the enemy's eyes. His receding hairline. The spittle flying from his mouth as he shouted at them.

Everything.

His finger tightened as he took aim.

She raised her weapon and pulled the trigger.

The impact knocked him backward, and his chest bloomed red as he fell into the dirt.

Time jumped to normal. She turned from the body. Her first kill. And probably not her last.

The butterflies in her stomach took flight.

She refocused her attention on the rest of the men firing from the shadows.

A bullet hit the back of Xavier's seat, sending packing everywhere and jarring Xavier."

"Xavier!" Bethany screamed his name.

He didn't even glance at her but kept his attention on the road ahead and on the men coming at them.

That was too close. Lips pressed tight, Bethany pivoted on her knees. A soldier chased them.

Bastard. She fired. Missed. *Breathe.* She took a deep breath, focused on the man—

And he fell sideways, grabbing the mangled flesh that was once his thigh.

"What the hell?" Bethany took her finger off the trigger, confused. She hadn't fired. But someone had. And from the jungle.

Eva?

Xavier veered right and Bethany's cap flew off, leaving her hair to whip in the wind. She shoved the tangled strands aside, staring into the dark, but whoever had helped her—saved Xavier—was gone.

Was it Eva? She wasn't sure. But who else could it have been?

More movement behind them drew her attention as soldiers ran for the wired jeeps. "Drive faster!" Bethany shouted, not sure how much explosives Xavier had used to rig the other vehicles. Would the explosion take out the compound or just the jeeps?

"Almost there," Xavier shouted back.

Seconds later, they cleared the gauntlet and found themselves on the dark, rutted path that served as a road. Xavier flicked on the headlights.

Behind them, there was a roar and a ball of fire rose in the night sky. Men ran and shouted, but the explosion was small and localized.

Anyone else was safe, including the hostages.

"Yes!" Bethany punched the sky as they turned a bend in the road, and the camp disappeared from sight leaving an orange glow on the edge of the tree line.

She flopped back in the seat, allowing herself a small smile. It wasn't a total win, but they'd hurt FARC and the hostages were alive. And with life there was hope.

Xavier slowed the jeep. "Any wounds?"

"I managed to dodge the bullets," she said. "How about you?"

"I'm all right," he said.

But no matter what he claimed, he wasn't all right. He wasn't even in the vicinity of "all right."

Bethany leaned back in the seat, an arm over her eyes, shaking with adrenaline. The fight was over, and they'd won the battle. Together, they'd saved her sister. Escaped the bad guys.

And lost Eva.

It was the last bit that struck Xavier harder and deeper than any bullet. And there was nothing she could do or say to save him from that pain.

"Wake up."

Bethany opened her eyes at Xavier's voice. They were parked on a ridge with open sky in front of them. The horizon was pink, and the birds in the trees behind them screamed and screeched as the sun rose over the jungle.

She sucked in cool air, loving the sky, the open air and anything that wasn't green and mossy. "Where are we?" she asked, stretching.

Xavier handed her the binoculars. "Take a look at the valley."

Tents. Campfires. Military vehicles. "Captain Veron's camp?"

"Not many other options," Xavier replied.

Last night, as she'd fallen asleep and Xavier drove, she'd thought they'd won the battle. But she hadn't felt it. She couldn't feel it until she was sure Samantha was safe.

And now…

Bethany scanned the camp, desperate for a sign of her sister. Other than the sentries, there was no movement.

"Do you think they made it?" The binoculars slipped from her fingers to her lap. What if they'd failed? What if Samantha and her protectors were captured? "We should go check. I can't see anything from here."

"My guess is that they are still asleep." He put in an earpiece and handed one to her. "Sebastian? Tomas? You there? Come back."

Static answered.

Bethany squeezed her eyes shut.

Xavier patted her hand. "Sebastian. Tomas. Wake the hell up."

"Ese." Sleep clouded Sebastian's voice, but she'd recognize it anywhere. "You made it back. What the hell happened?"

Xavier leaned back in the seat and looked sideways at Bethany. "It's a long story."

"Does it involve explosions?"

"Of course," Xavier replied. "That can wait. Where's Samantha?"

"Please," Bethany cut in. "Is she there? Is she okay?"

"Right here. She wouldn't let them separate her from us. Bethany," his voice dropped to a whisper, "I think she has a little crush on Tomas."

"I heard that," Tomas said.

Bethany could almost hear him blush. "Duke it out later, boys. Can I speak to her?"

Seconds ticked by and anxiety twisted her stomach into knots. "Where are they?"

"Bethany? Can you hear me?"

Samantha's voice rang in her ear and all curiosity was lost in her relief at hearing her sister's voice. "I hear you loud and clear," Bethany said as two-years' worth of tears filled her eyes. Her sister was free. Safe. They were a family again.

For a long while, she'd thought this day might never arrive. "Are they treating you right?" she asked, sniffing.

"I'm fine. Captain Veron was a little wary when we showed up, but once he realized I'd been a hostage, he was great."

"How about it, guys?" Xavier asked. "Is he buying the story? That you found her?"

"Not at all. He was pissed once he figured out that Samantha is Bethany's sister," Tomas explained.

Bethany couldn't blame him. No one liked to be made the fool.

Tomas continued, "He's cool now. He'll take the credit for the rescue and we'll call it even."

"I'm good with that," Bethany said. He could have whatever he wanted as far as she was concerned.

"Bethany?" Samantha's voice cracked with tension. "Where are you? When do I get to see you?"

Bethany looked down over the valley. "We're close." She wiped her cheeks, smiling through the tears.

There was a rustling on the other end. "They're coming to bring us breakfast," Samantha said. "Tomas says I have to go. They don't want Veron to know about the earpieces."

"Okay, I'll see you soon," Bethany said. "I love you."

"I love you, too."

The static returned.

Bethany pulled off the earpiece and let it fall to the floor. "Thank you," she whispered.

"You're welcome," Xavier said.

She watched the sky lighten above them. It was a new day and a new life for her and Samantha.

But not for Xavier. The man who deserved a happy ending

as much as, if not more than, anyone else. "I'm sorry that you didn't get Eva back."

He nodded. "Me, too."

The apology wasn't enough. There were things that needed to be said. Things Xavier needed to know. "She saved us. I thought you should know."

Xavier's brows knit together. "How so?"

"I was aiming for the man behind us, and I missed. She took him out before I got a second shot and kept him from firing again."

"I'll keep it in mind," he said. She saw appreciation in his gaze. But no absolution.

"It's not enough to forgive her, is it?" Bethany muttered.

He shook his head. "She took hostages. She threatened you. She betrayed our people and our cause. I let her live. That is all the forgiveness I can offer her."

"She betrayed you," Bethany said, knowing where the conversion had to go. "Like I did."

With a sigh, Xavier opened the door of the vehicle, got out and paced its length. "You lied to me, Bethany. Used me."

There was no reason to deny the obvious.

Xavier continued, "I am not going to say it was all right. It is never all right to use someone like that." He stopped pacing. "But I understand why."

Bethany's breath caught in her throat. "I am so sorry. I took from you and hid the truth. I should have said something sooner."

"You were selfish."

She nodded, keeping her head down, not wanting to see the disappointment in his eyes. "I was."

"You were scared."

She buried her face in her hands. "I was so scared." Her voice broke, regret overwhelming her. "I didn't want to lose Samantha. Then I didn't want to lose you. I knew I had to give up one or the other. It was stupid and foolish, and I should have told you everything. Let you make that choice." She looked up at him, willing him to believe her.

She continued, "But I didn't. I kept up the lie even after I knew I could trust you with *anything*. With my *life*. I am so sorry." She reached out to him. "I wish I could take it all back."

Xavier took her hand, pulled her from the jeep and into his arms.

Bethany inhaled him. He smelled like the jungle. Like sweat. Like everything she ever wanted.

"Not *all* back," Xavier whispered, his mouth pressed against her hair. "Not you. Not us."

Fear whispered for her to remain silent. To not ask what she didn't want to know. Bethany shook the fear away. She'd let it make her decisions before and she'd be damned if she'd do that again. She might not like the answer, but she'd take it. Whatever it was.

"There's still an us?" she asked.

He smoothed her hair back. "I thought a lot last night while you slept. Mostly about something Eva said. That forgiveness should not have strings."

He sighed. "My sister is confused right now. I don't know why and I can't fix it. But she was right about that. Either I forgive or I don't.

"I forgive you, Bethany." He kissed the top of her head. "And there will always be an us. Always."

Bethany pressed her face into Xavier's chest. She didn't deserve this. This easy forgiveness. But she'd take it and be grateful. "Thank you."

"Don't thank me yet. You'll be stubborn. I'll get frustrated. I am sure it will be a bumpy ride."

Bethany looked into Xavier's eyes and saw something she'd never seen before. A future.

She grinned. "Stubborn? Me?"

"Yes. You." He grinned back and this time, it went all the

way to his eyes. "But there will be forgiveness, as well. For both of us. No strings."

It was a heady thought. But she wanted more. And this time, she wasn't going to let fear keep her silent. "And love?"

"And love." Xavier brushed his lips against hers. "I promise."

Epilogue

"Moss is going to grow on me if I don't move soon," Bethany muttered.

"You talk too much," Xavier said.

Wearing camouflage and paint, she and Xavier lay next to each other, watching Cesar and his men in the valley below.

Through the binoculars, she watched the FARC leader emerge from his hut. Arms waving and bald head shining in the sun, he shouted orders and then backhanded a hostage.

New camp. New location. *Same jerk.*

Bethany frowned. It had taken them six months and a lot of inquiries, but she, Xavier and his team were fulfilling their promise to her sister—they were rescuing the other hostages. Today, if all went as planned.

Her mother had pitched a fit when Bethany told her that she was returning to Colombia with Xavier, but it was her home now. It was where she was needed.

And it was what Samantha needed. Still in therapy, two years as a hostage had changed her little sister. She acted as if she were better. She smiled. Said and did all the right things.

But that was a show Samantha put on for the sake of Bethany and their mother. Bethany couldn't ignore Samantha's cries at night or the shrieks when nightmares woke her. She couldn't turn away from the pain that her sister fought to hide. Samantha might act as if she was healing, but her inner demons still held her in their grip.

But at least she *had* Samantha.

Eva had never returned and there had been no word of Xavier's sister in the past six months.

She'd tried to talk to him about her, but he refused.

Maybe one day…

But it would have to be when he was ready.

Bethany glanced at her watch and sighed. "Seriously, what's taking them so long?"

"Be patient," Xavier suggested, watching the camp.

She flicked a bug off her wrist. "Patience was never my virtue."

"Nice excuse, but I know better," Xavier replied, ignoring her agitation.

It was true. She had learned patience over the past few months and that skill had helped save them. Building and rebuilding her relationship with Xavier hadn't happened over night. There had been more talking. A few fights. And great makeup sex.

"There's a lot to be said for makeup sex."

Xavier froze then looked at her, his expression confused. "Where did that come from?"

She grinned. "Nothing."

Xavier rolled his eyes and went back to watching the camp.

Yes, patience had paid off.

They'd weathered the hard time and came out stronger. She clasped Xavier's hand in hers. "Have I told you how happy you make me?"

Eyes still on the movement below, Xavier smiled. "You have. Except when we're out here."

Bethany grinned. "You make me happy." She flicked another bug. "Bugs creep me out."

"You can go back," Xavier suggested.

"You wish." It was their one constant battle—his desire to keep her safe and her desire to be the person who did the right thing.

He shrugged in response.

"You don't want to fight about it?" Bethany pressed, a little disappointed at his easy acquiescence.

Xavier's smiled morphed into a grin. "You just want great makeup sex."

Mr. Funny-man. She chuckled. "And would you turn me down?"

"You two ready to make some noise?" Sebastian's voice came over Bethany's earpiece before Xavier could respond. "We're in position and ready to move."

"Ready," she replied, Xavier's answer mixing with hers.

"Do what I say." Xavier set the binoculars down, all humor gone and his eyes boring into her. "And be careful."

"Of course," Bethany said, shaking as adrenaline rushed through her. "I'm always careful." She took a deep breath. This was it—her first rescue.

She rolled away to rise but Xavier gabbed her arm and rolled her back.

"What now?" she asked.

Xavier cradled her head in his hands, so they were face-to-face. "I'm serious. Be careful. I don't want to lose you."

She heard the fear in his voice and felt it in his touch. She recognized it because she felt the same fear when she thought of him on a mission without her. Not that she was a talisman capable of keeping him safe, but if he were wounded, her place wasn't sitting at his bar, waiting.

It was at his side. It didn't matter if they were crossing a gorge on a zip-line, freeing hostages or waking up in the morning. They were partners. Lovers. A team. And there wasn't enough fear in the world to change that.

Leaning in, she kissed him. He returned the kiss, his mouth warm. She breathed him in. "You will never lose me. I promise."

* * * * *

**We'll be spotlighting a different series
every month throughout 2009
to celebrate our 60th anniversary.**

Look for Silhouette® Nocturne™ in October!

Travel through time to experience tales
that reach the boundaries of life and death.
Bestselling authors Lindsay McKenna, Cindy
Dees, P.C. Cast and Merline Lovelace join
together in a brand-new, four-book
Time Raiders miniseries.

TIME RAIDERS

August—*The Seeker*
by *USA TODAY* bestselling author Lindsay McKenna

September—*The Slayer* by Cindy Dees

October—*The Avenger*
by *New York Times* bestselling author and
coauthor of the House of Night novels P.C. Cast

November—*The Protector*
by *USA TODAY* bestselling author Merline Lovelace

Available wherever books are sold.

nocturne™

New York Times bestselling author
and co-author of the House of Night novels

P.C. CAST

makes her stellar debut
in Silhouette® Nocturne™

THE AVENGER

Available October wherever books are sold.

TIME RAIDERS
miniseries

Bestselling authors Lindsay McKenna,
Cindy Dees, P.C. Cast and Merline Lovelace
come together to bring to life incredible
tales of passion that reach the boundaries
of life and death, in a brand-new
four-book miniseries.

REQUEST YOUR FREE BOOKS!

2 FREE NOVELS PLUS 2 FREE GIFTS!

V *Silhouette®* Romantic

SUSPENSE

Sparked by Danger, Fueled by Passion!

YES! Please send me 2 FREE Silhouette® Romantic Suspense novels and my 2 FREE gifts (gifts are worth about $10). After receiving them, if I don't wish to receive any more books, I can return the shipping statement marked "cancel." If I don't cancel, I will receive 4 brand-new novels every month and be billed just $4.24 per book in the U.S. or $4.99 per book in Canada. That's a savings of at least 15% off the cover price! It's quite a bargain! Shipping and handling is just 50¢ per book*. I understand that accepting the 2 free books and gifts places me under no obligation to buy anything. I can always return a shipment and cancel at any time. Even if I never buy another book from Silhouette, the two free books and gifts are mine to keep forever.

240 SDN EYL4 340 SDN EYMG

Name	(PLEASE PRINT)

Address	Apt. #

City	State/Prov.	Zip/Postal Code

Signature (if under 18, a parent or guardian must sign)

Mail to the Silhouette Reader Service:
IN U.S.A.: P.O. Box 1867, Buffalo, NY 14240-1867
IN CANADA: P.O. Box 609, Fort Erie, Ontario L2A 5X3

Not valid to current subscribers of Silhouette Romantic Suspense books.

Want to try two free books from another line?
Call 1-800-873-8635 or visit www.morefreebooks.com.

* Terms and prices subject to change without notice. Prices do not include applicable taxes. Sales tax applicable in N.Y. Canadian residents will be charged applicable provincial taxes and GST. Offer not valid in Quebec. This offer is limited to one order per household. All orders subject to approval. Credit or debit balances in a customer's account(s) may be offset by any other outstanding balance owed by or to the customer. Please allow 4 to 6 weeks for delivery. Offer available while quantities last.

Your Privacy: Silhouette is committed to protecting your privacy. Our Privacy Policy is available online at www.eHarlequin.com or upon request from the Reader Service. From time to time we make our lists of customers available to reputable third parties who may have a product or service of interest to you. If you would prefer we not share your name and address, please check here. ☐

SRS09R

In 2009 Harlequin celebrates
60 years of pure reading pleasure!

We're marking this occasion by offering
16 **FREE** full books to download and read.

Visit

www.HarlequinCelebrates.com

to choose from a variety of
great romance stories
that are absolutely **FREE!**

(Total approximate retail value of $60)

We invite you to visit and share the Web site
with your friends, family
and anyone who enjoys reading.

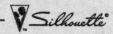

SPECIAL EDITION

FROM *NEW YORK TIMES* BESTSELLING AUTHOR

SUSAN MALLERY

THE SHEIK AND THE BOUGHT BRIDE

Victoria McCallan works in Prince Kateb's palace. When Victoria's gambling father is caught cheating at cards with the prince, Victoria saves her father from going to jail by being Kateb's mistress for six months. But the darkly handsome desert sheik isn't as harsh as Victoria thinks he is, and Kateb finds himself attracted to his new mistress. But Kateb has already loved and lost once—is he willing to give love another try?

Available in October wherever books are sold.

SSE65481

Visit Silhouette Books at www.eHarlequin.com